WITH ALL MY HEART

Germany, 1938. Anti-Jewish feeling is increasing and when Miriam and Rebekah's parents are killed in a bomb attack, the girls are snatched from their lives of wealth and privilege to be abandoned in an orphanage. There, the sisters meet fellow Jew, Karl, and the three young people are assisted out of Germany on the Kindertransport train. Miriam and Karl feel a connection but circumstances part them before they reach England. How can they possibly find each other again?

DAWN KNOX

WITH ALL MY HEART

Complete and Unabridged

LINFORD
Leicester

First published in Great Britain in 2019

First Linford Edition
published 2020

A catalogue record for this book is available
from the British Library.

ISBN 978–1–4448–4622–5

Published by
Ulverscroft Limited
Anstey, Leicestershire

Set by Words & Graphics Ltd.
Anstey, Leicestershire
Printed and bound in Great Britain by
T. J. International Ltd., Padstow, Cornwall

This book is printed on acid-free paper

1

1938 Cologne, Germany

Some said it had been a tragic accident. New gas ovens had been fitted in the kitchens of the exclusive Königskrone Klub the day before, ready for the owner's birthday celebrations on the evening of the third of February. At some point, emphasis had shifted from safety to speed.

Others said it had been a bomb.

People gathered — many with coats over their nightclothes — at either end of Königstraße, surveying the broken glass that littered the street and gazing with open mouths at the enormous flames which licked the night sky.

Many theories about the cause were expressed. Some remarked that it had been a coincidence that the explosion occurred as the church bells chimed eleven o'clock, as if it had been timed.

Of course, there was the question of the guests at the banquet. They would mostly, or indeed all, have been Jews except for the kitchen staff and waiters. The owner of the Königskrone Klub, Jacob Littauer, had made his money in banking and was known to have many Jewish colleagues and friends — all rich, but none as wealthy as him.

'Think of all those families, broken apart,' lamented one woman.

'It's no loss. They're just Jews,' a man replied.

'That's a terrible thing to say! They've probably got children waiting at home.'

'So what? They'll have nannies and servants.'

'You obviously don't have children of your own, or you wouldn't be so heartless,' the woman said and others in the crowd nodded in agreement.

'They're just Jews,' the man repeated. 'They steal what's ours. They take from our children.'

'There'll be diamonds in the ash,' a

woman said. 'It might be worth coming back tomorrow.'

'Diamonds burn like anything else,' a man said. 'There won't be much left after that blaze.'

The crowd began to surge from behind, as a group of police officers fought their way through. They pushed the onlookers back down the street.

'Move along. Make way for the fire engines,' one policeman shouted. 'Nothing to see here!'

A gust fanned the flames and chased the smoke along Königstraße. There was another explosion and clouds of dust rolled towards the crowd. People broke away to return home.

'The fire engines took their time arriving,' one woman commented.

'Why should our men risk their lives for those bloodsuckers?' someone replied.

2

Across the city, in one of the grander mansions in Eichestraße, Miriam awoke. The clock on her bedside table showed five past eleven and she wondered what had roused her.

Perhaps Mutter and Vater had come home? But surely not. It was much too early. She knew they didn't usually return from an evening out until the small hours — sometimes not until first light.

And tonight, they would definitely not be early. She'd begged Mutter to allow her to go to Uncle Jacob's birthday party at the Königskrone Klub.

'Not this year, Liebling.'

'But Mutter, I'm nearly sixteen! Surely a few weeks won't matter?'

Frau Rosenberg had patted Miriam's head.

'No, Liebling. Not this year. Your birthday is more than a few weeks away.

Anyway, Rebekah needs you. I'm sorry. But I promise you shall come with Vater and me next year.'

Miriam had sighed. A year was such a long time. But Mutter was right; her sister, Rebekah, was a highly-strung child and often sleep-walked. Miriam seemed to be the only person who could calm her sister when she woke and found herself somewhere other than her bed. Next year, Rebekah would be ten. Surely by then, she'd have outgrown her nervousness.

Putting on a robe, Miriam tiptoed out of her bedroom. Pressing her ear to Rebekah's bedroom door, she listened but there was just the sound of regular breathing.

She crept towards her parents' bedroom. Perhaps Mutter had one of her headaches and they'd returned early after all. But the door was ajar and Miriam could see the room was empty.

She slipped in and warmed herself in front of the fire. Traces of Chanel No 5 hung in the air with the scent of face powder, taking Miriam back to the early evening when Elsa had dressed Mutter in her new satin gown. The maid had been with the family for as long as Miriam could remember and somehow knew exactly what Mutter would need next during the long process of dressing.

Miriam sat on the bed watching the satin gown being slipped over her mother's head and the beautiful diamond jewellery being fastened around her neck and wrists. When Mutter was satisfied with her hair, make-up and dress, she'd taken the square bottle and removing the stopper, she'd dabbed the perfume on her wrists and behind her ears.

Miriam moved to the dressing table and, lifting the bottle, she carefully withdrew the stopper and mimicked her mother's actions. The fragrance surrounded her and she wondered if Mutter would notice and be angry when she returned.

She'd just decided to open a window

to allow some of the wonderful scent to dissipate when she heard the sound of sirens screaming somewhere across Cologne. Seconds later, Rebekah's door opened.

Miriam rushed out in to the corridor.

'Bekah? I'm here, Liebling,' she called softly. 'No need to worry.'

'What's that terrible sound, Mirrie?'

'It's just a siren somewhere. Nothing for you to worry about. Go back to bed.'

'Can I come in with you?'

'Yes, of course. Let's go to my bed. Come on, before we both catch cold.' Miriam put her arm round the small girl's shoulders.

'I can smell Mutter's perfume,' Rebekah said, 'are she and Vater home?'

'No, Liebling, they're still at Uncle Jacob's party. I expect they'll still be a while yet.'

Miriam settled Rebekah and then crept in beside her, placing her arm over her protectively. Within seconds, Rebekah was asleep.

★ ★ ★

It seemed to Miriam she'd hardly closed her eyes when Elsa threw open the door without knocking and rushed into the bedroom.

'Oh, Miss, the police are here. They're asking for you and Miss Rebekah.'

'Police? For us? Why haven't you woken Mutter and Vater?'

The maid clutched her apron tightly, her mouth opening and closing as she struggled to find the right words.

'What's the matter?' asked Rebekah sleepily.

'Nothing to worry about, Liebling, I'll go and find out.'

'Where are you going, Mirrie?' Rebekah asked.

'Just downstairs. I'm sure it's a mistake. Go back to sleep.'

Miriam put on her robe and followed the maid.

At the bottom of the sweeping staircase stood three policemen. Two looked down at their boots, their helmets tucked under their arms, obviously ill at ease in such a wealthy home.

The third man, however, had not removed his helmet. He stepped forward, his chin jutting out belligerently and his expression arrogant. The housekeeper, clutching the arm of the butler, stood nearby, wearing expressions of shock.

Miriam stopped halfway down the stairs.

'Can I help you, gentlemen?' she asked with a clear and steady voice, in the way she knew Mutter would have done had she been there.

'Fräulein Rosenberg?' asked the policeman.

'Yes, I am Miriam Rosenberg. How can I help you?'

'I'm afraid I have some bad news,' he said curtly. 'Your parents were involved in an accident last night at the Königskrone Klub. And . . . '

Miriam held on to the banister to steady herself.

'Can my sister and I go to them?'

'That will not be possible. They were

involved in an explosion. They are dead. Along with everyone else who was at the party. Their bodies have not been recovered and are not likely to be.'

The housekeeper shrieked, her hands flying to her mouth.

'Was that necessary?' The butler stepped forward. 'There are surely kinder ways of letting a young girl know her . . . her . . . parents have . . . '

Unabashed, the policeman addressed Miriam.

'You and your sister have fifteen minutes to pack a small bag each. Then you will accompany me.' He turned to the butler. 'You will dismiss the servants and pack your things. This house has been confiscated by the authorities.'

For a few seconds, no one moved.

'C . . . confiscated?' stammered the butler.

'We have orders to seize the property of anyone suspected of being a political enemy of the state.'

'There's obviously some mistake. My parents aren't political enemies of the state!' said Miriam.

'They aren't now, but when they were alive, they were,' the officer said nastily. 'You now have fourteen minutes until you are escorted from the property.' He peeled off a glove and checked his wrist watch. 'Soon, you will only have thirteen.'

Elsa was first to react. Taking Miriam's hand, she pulled her up the stairs. Flinging open her wardrobe, she pulled two suitcases off the top shelf and started filling one of them with the warmest clothing she could find.

Miriam ran to the bed and put her arm round Rebekah. She must remain strong. Mutter and Vater couldn't possibly be . . . She couldn't bear to form the word in her mind, let alone speak it.

'It's just a mistake,' she said to Rebekah. 'It'll be sorted out soon but, in the meantime, we have to go out. Can you do that for me, Liebling?'

Rebekah began to sob. She clung to her sister, sensing the drama but unable to understand.

11

Elsa ran out of the room, returning seconds later with Frau Rosenberg's jewellery box. Opening it, she tipped everything on top of Miriam's clothes.

'This isn't the most valuable stuff, Miss Miriam, but I don't know the combination for the safe and there's no time. Please, Miss, I know it's a shock but you have to help me! Here are some clothes. Please get dressed, then take this case and fill it with Miss Rebekah's warmest things. Go! Now!'

Miriam stood up, took the case and garments and led her sister back to her room. She dressed, then helped Rebekah put on a thick, woollen frock and did as the maid had told her, filling the case with all the warm clothes she could find. Then kneeling on the lid to squeeze everything inside, she pushed the clasps home.

Elsa met them in the corridor, took the case from Miriam and then grasped Rebekah's hand.

'I haven't packed Ralf!' Miriam stopped.

'There's no time, Miss! Go downstairs, please! Don't upset that man. He's trouble.'

Ignoring the maid, Miriam rushed back to her sister's room to retrieve the teddy bear. When she reached the bottom of the stairs, the servants were standing in the hall holding bundles and cases, looking anxiously at the butler for direction. Judging by the sounds of drawers being ripped out and books being overturned, the two junior officers were searching Herr Rosenberg's study.

'Good,' said the officer tapping his watch, 'you have not made me wait. All you servants can go.'

The butler nodded. They turned as one, heading for the servants' entrance.

'That way!' roared the policeman, pointing at the front door. 'You don't have to observe the social niceties now. The Jewish dogs are gone.'

The housekeeper gasped with shock.

'You should be ashamed of yourself!' she said.

The policeman lashed out with his

leather glove, catching her across the face. The butler took her arm, quickly steering her away.

'Jew-lovers!' the officer said and spat on the Persian rug. Turning back to the Rosenberg girls, his lip curled in contempt, he saw Elsa still there.

'I told you to go! The Jew girls have no need of a maid where they're going. Now get out before I arrest you too!'

Elsa turned to go upstairs.

'Out!' the man bellowed, pointing at the door.

'Please, Sir, I need to pack my things. They're upstairs in my room.'

'You had your chance. Now, get out!'

Miriam stepped towards the man.

'Please let her get her things. She was helping my sister and me pack — '

'Enough!' The man hit Miriam with the back of his hand. 'She chose to assist an enemy of the state, so now she forfeits her things. Get out!' he said to the trembling maid, his voice menacing.

Miriam watched as Elsa hurried across the marble floor and opened the front door. A chilly draught blew in as she slipped out without her coat or belongings into the cold February morning.

This simply can't be happening, thought Miriam. In a world which had always been organised and genteel, this madness was beyond belief. Something would surely happen which would restore normality.

Next to her, Rebekah whimpered and Miriam passed her a handkerchief.

Please don't cry, Rebekah, she thought, *please don't do anything to anger this mad man.*

As if reading her mind, her sister held the handkerchief to her mouth, stifling the sobs.

Leaving the two junior officers with orders to search the mansion and guard it, in case the servants had access to keys and returned, the policeman propelled the two girls roughly towards the waiting police car.

'No talking!' he said as he pushed them into the back of the car, where they clung to each other in silence. He climbed into the passenger seat and the driver started the engine.

Further along the road, several of their servants stood watching the police vehicle, although they walked rapidly towards the corner when it approached them and were soon lost from sight.

There was such a sense of unreality that it appeared to Miriam as if everything was happening in slow motion. Neighbours' curtains fluttered and in several Jewish homes, they were hastily drawn together as if the action would keep marauders from their houses. A few strangers had gathered, and several had hands in front of their mouths as they spoke. However, fingers pointing at the Rosenberg's house betrayed the topic of conversation.

One angry-looking man shook his fist at the car as it passed. Miriam had heard of attacks against Jews in other cities but Mutter had assured her they were a few isolated incidents carried out by misguided individuals. Now she wondered if her mother hadn't been trying to shield her from a very unpleasant truth. But surely Mutter wouldn't have deliberately misled her?

Miriam craned her neck to look back at the house where she and Rebekah had grown up. One of the police officers stood on the doorstep, feet apart, hands clasped behind his back facing the small crowd which still waited and watched from the other side of the road. As they turned the corner, a wave of desolation washed over her.

'Why is this happening to us, Mirrie?' Rebekah whispered. Miriam held a finger to her lips, warning her sister not to anger the policeman in the front. And anyway, she had no answer.

At the police station, the girls were taken to a cell by a custody officer.

'Are you locking us up?' Miriam asked incredulously.

'It's for your own protection,' he said. 'Probably only for one night, until arrangements are made.'

Some time later, he brought two

chipped and stained mugs of hot, unsweetened tea and chunks of bread.

'Please, Sir,' Miriam said hesitantly, 'would it be possible to have our suitcases?'

'As soon as they've been searched.'

'Searched? What for?'

He shrugged and muttered something as he closed the door. His huge bunch of keys jangled as he selected the correct one and turned it.

When he came back with their cases, Miriam opened hers, taking out some clothes to put on one of the narrow beds to make it more comfortable. There were two beds in the cell but she knew her sister wouldn't sleep on her own. Each mattress was barely wide enough for one but Rebekah was small for her age and they could probably squeeze on together.

The thought of a night in this fetid, windowless room which was hardly larger than one of the storage cupboards in her parents' house was terrifying. As soon as the stark light bulb was turned off, it would be pitch black. Or perhaps, it wouldn't be turned out at all. Who knew what was going to happen? But at least they were together — at the moment — and the thought of holding Rebekah close was strangely comforting.

Miriam opened her case and selected several skirts to roll up as pillows. It wasn't until she came across one of Mutter's pearl earrings caught in the suitcase lining that she realised all the jewellery Elsa had packed with her clothes earlier was missing. All except this one piece. She held the single pearl tightly in her fist and thought of her mother. If only it had occurred to her to bring a photograph of her parents. If only . . .

'When will Mutter and Vater come for us?' Rebekah asked. 'Vater will be so angry with that horrible policeman, won't he, Mirrie? He called us such nasty names. And how uncouth to spit on the rug! D'you think Vater will have him dismissed from the police? It would serve him right.'

The breath caught in Miriam's throat.

Rebekah still didn't know about their parents. She'd been upstairs waiting for her and Elsa to return when the officer had so cruelly announced their fate.

'Liebling,' Miriam said, putting her arms round her sister. 'You must try to be very grown-up now because I have some bad news. When that horrible man came to our house . . . he said . . . '

Miriam tried to pick her words carefully but there was no kind way of telling her sister they were now orphans. When she'd finished, she expected a torrent of tears but Rebekah sat in silence, staring ahead.

'Liebling?' Miriam said, anxious at her sister's lack of response. 'You mustn't worry. I'll look after you.' She knelt in front of Rebekah, taking her hands. They both knew it was a hollow promise.

Miriam coaxed Rebekah to eat the soup and bread the custody officer brought. They hadn't eaten all day although neither girl was hungry.

When he took the bowls away, the man warned them the light would go out in fifteen minutes, at ten o'clock.

They lay on the hard, narrow mattress, Miriam with her back to the tiled wall and her arm over Rebekah, holding her close. A little over twelve hours ago, they'd been lying in the comfort of her bed, unaware their world was about to shatter.

Twelve hours! She couldn't account for much of it and wondered if she'd lost consciousness. Or perhaps her mind had simply not been able to take everything in and had coped by going blank.

Rebekah lay rigid in her arms, clutching her teddy bear. She was obviously in shock but Miriam didn't know what to do or say.

'Mirrie? Are you awake?'

'Yes, Liebling.' Miriam made her voice calm.

'This bed smells horrible.'

Suddenly Miriam had an idea. She moved her arm so that her wrist was near Rebekah's nose.

'I can smell Mutter's perfume, Mirrie,' Rebekah said.

'It's what I dabbed on my wrists last night.'

'Will you leave your wrist there?'

'Yes, of course.'

A hint of Chanel No 5 wafted towards Miriam. She inhaled deeply, not wanting the fragrance to evaporate and vanish. She felt Rebekah's chest rise and fall as she too breathed in the scent

'Is this all that's left of Mutter?'

Miriam's throat constricted.

'I don't think I can bear it, Mirrie,' Rebekah said and at last, she gave way to grief, her tiny body heaving as she sobbed.

★　★　★

The jangle of keys outside woke the two girls and seconds later, the electric light lit up the tiny cell with a harsh light. Miriam ached from lying in one position on the hard mattress all night. Her eyes were swollen with crying and her cheek was bruised and red where the policeman had hit her the previous day when she'd asked for permission for Elsa to pack her things.

The night before, when Rebekah had started to cry, Miriam could no longer hold back her tears. Eventually, they'd both fallen into an exhausted sleep, punctuated only by the drunken shouts and curses from one of the other police cells.

The custody officer entered with two bowls of porridge and two mugs of tea.

'Someone will be back for you shortly,' he said.

'Where are we going?' Miriam asked, her voice hoarse from crying.

'St Josef's Orphanage.' His tone was matter of fact but his eyes were gentle.

The porridge was cold, lumpy and glutinous but they were hungry, so they forced it down.

'It's like the paste I use for my scrapbook,' said Rebekah, her eyes filling with tears again as she remembered the carefully compiled collections which had been left behind.

'Perhaps where we're going, we'll be

able to get you a new scrapbook,' said Miriam.

'Will one of Vater's friends come for us?'

'I'm not sure,' Miriam said, knowing it was unlikely. Most of their parents' friends had been at Uncle Jacob's party.

'What about Uncle Reuben?'

'He lives in Boston, Liebling. I don't suppose he even knows where we are.'

'Can we write to him?'

'Yes — I will, as soon as I can.'

It was best that Rebekah clung to that hope. As soon as she could, Miriam would write but she wasn't sure she could remember Uncle Reuben's address. It was either 1128 or 1218 Fairburn Street. Or was it 1281?

Well, as soon as she had paper and envelopes, she'd send the same letter to all three houses. Uncle Reuben, her father's younger brother, had emigrated to America several years ago. Just before he left, he argued with Vater and it was only because Mutter had periodically written to her brother-in-law, hoping that one day the rift would be healed, that Miriam had seen her uncle's address. Surely once he knew of his nieces' situation, he'd come back to Germany and find them — argument or no argument.

Miriam felt more positive now she had a plan.

'How long before the policeman comes back for us?' Rebekah asked.

Miriam looked at her watch and realised she'd forgotten to wind it. It had stopped.

'I don't know, Liebling. It can't be much longer.'

'How are we going to wash, Mirrie?'

Miriam shook her head. 'Perhaps we'll be able to wash when we get to wherever they're taking us.' She felt grimy and her mouth tasted stale and gluey after the gelatinous porridge. As for her hair, she knew it was tangled and unkempt. Usually so proud of her thick, wavy black hair, she attempted to comb it with her fingers. Rebekah's glossy, straight hair was now lank and lifeless and Miriam did her best to smooth it into shape.

When the custody officer eventually arrived for them, the girls were sitting on the bed, side by side, dressed in their coats, cases on their laps.

'Follow me,' he said in an indifferent tone. His eyes, however, betrayed the softness Miriam thought she'd detected before. Taking her hand, he pressed two coins in her palm.

'One each,' he said gruffly. 'Now, put 'em in your pocket and when you get the chance, slip 'em into your shoe. It ain't much . . . And don't tell anyone where you got 'em.'

Before putting them in her pocket, Miriam glanced at the two, small bronze coins, each worth two Reichspfennigs.

'Thank you,' she said as if the man had given her a handful of gold.

She'd never had any need to handle money before. Household accounts were settled by the housekeeper. Mutter had never carried money and there'd been no need for Miriam to have any either. At one time she probably wouldn't have bothered to pick up a two-pfennig coin if she'd seen one on the ground. But she recognised that the coins were of value to the kind custody officer and that in their new predicament, they were going to be important to her and Rebekah too.

The girls were relieved to see the officer who was to accompany them was not the one who'd come to their house the previous day.

'It should only take about ten minutes,' the officer said over his shoulder to the girls who were sitting on the back seat holding hands.

Miriam looked out of the window. She recognised nothing and could scarcely believe they were still in Cologne, but they were only a short distance from the police station.

They were used to main streets lined with expensive shops, cafés and restaurants and was familiar with the museums and theatres, but the side streets they were travelling along now were lined with ugly, shabby buildings which she realised were not single houses like her parents' home in Eichestraße, but apartment blocks which judging by the washing on display from various windows, contained many rooms in which an enormous number of people lived. Ragged children and scruffy dogs played in the street among overflowing rubbish bins. Miriam had never seen anything like it and the further they went, the more dilapidated the buildings became.

Finally, the car turned into St-Josef-Straße and pulled up at a grimy, red brick building that would once have been rather elegant. Now, a faded sign announced *St Josef's Orphanage*.

3

A small, bird-like woman stood at the door cradling a baby in one arm, her other hand on the head of a small child who held on to her apron. She smiled as Miriam and Rebekah climbed out of the car with their suitcases.

'Two more, Sister Margarete,' the policeman said as he handed the woman a large envelope. He leaned towards her and said something in her ear which Miriam thought might have been *Jews*.

Sister Margarete looked back at her and Rebekah with a worried glance, but said firmly, 'All God's children are welcome under this roof.'

Without acknowledging the girls, the man got back in the car and it pulled away.

'Welcome to St Josef's, girls,' the woman said, her thin face lighting up with a smile. 'I am Sister Margarete.

Come in, come in.'

Miriam and Rebekah followed the woman who, despite her small stature, now had the child balanced on one hip as well as the baby on her arm. She led them through a dingy hall which smelled of damp wood and cabbage into a large kitchen where several children were working.

Sister Margarete placed the sleeping baby in a box and sat down, transferring the child who'd been riding on her hip to her lap. It played contentedly with the large cross she wore.

'Children! We have two new girls,' she announced. Opening the envelope, she read the details. 'We have Miriam and Rebekah Rosenberg. Please welcome them.'

Several of the children smiled, others nodded. No one seemed very interested.

'Shall I set two more places on the table for lunch?' one young girl asked, scowling at the sisters. 'There's hardly enough as it is.'

'We will make do, Greta,' Sister Margarete said, patting her on the head. 'Now, please keep an eye on the baby while I show our newcomers where they'll sleep.'

As she led the girls upstairs, she explained there were eleven children but two of the older boys would soon be leaving — after their fifteenth birthdays they would be required to work in the nearby mines. Several of the younger children went to school, and Sister Margarete told Rebekah she would join them on Monday.

'We'll find you a job,' she told Miriam. 'Do you have any skills?'

Miriam shook her head.

'No matter, we'll find you something, I'm sure.'

⋆ ⋆ ⋆

That night in their bed in the attic, the two girls whispered together.

'Do you have any paper to write to Uncle Reuben, Mirrie?'

'No, Liebling. I'll ask Sister Margarete tomorrow.'

'What sort of work will you have to do?'

31

Miriam sighed. 'Sister Margarete thinks she will be able to get me a position as a maid.'

'Like Elsa?' Rebekah was shocked. 'But you've never done any work. How will you know what to do?'

'I don't know. I'll just have to learn as I go.'

'When will you be able to write to Uncle Reuben, Mirrie? The sooner he knows about us, the sooner he'll come.'

'Yes, Liebling,' Miriam said, wondering if the four pfennigs which the kind policeman had given them would be enough to buy the stamps for a letter to America. When she'd lived with Mutter and Vater, servants had delivered letters or arranged to have them posted.

Miriam felt overwhelmed. There was so much she didn't know and had been shielded from.

'If Mutter was here, Mirrie, what d'you think she'd be telling us to do?' Rebekah whispered.

'Well . . . I think she might say we needed to keep our chins up and then

she'd say, 'There's always sunshine —''
'After a shower,' Rebekah finished.
'Yes, that's right.'
'Mirrie? Can you still smell Chanel No 5 on your wrist?'
'No, Liebling, I'm afraid it's worn off.'
'Mutter's really gone, hasn't she, Mirrie?'
Miriam couldn't speak for the lump in her throat.

★   ★   ★

'Tomorrow, we'll have been at St Josef's for a whole month, Mirrie,' Rebekah said, looking up from writing in her diary. It wasn't a real diary — the red leather book had been left behind in the house in Eichestraße, along with her scrapbooks. Miriam had been working for a family in a large house not far away and she'd rescued some paper from the waste bin to bring home for her sister. The corners had been accidentally folded over and Frau Wachtler, who was now Miriam's employer, had thrown the sheets out.

Rebekah had folded the sheets in half

and Sister Margarete had bound them together with a few stitches of brown wool. On the front of the diary, Rebekah had written in her neatest handwriting: *Rebekah Rosenberg. My Diary. Private. Keep Out.*

There were two pictures of butterflies stuck to the cover with flour and water paste.

Those butterflies had caused many problems for Miriam. She'd spotted them on the cover of a magazine which Frau Wachtler had thrown away. She'd torn the cover off, folding it carefully so as to keep the butterflies flat, and tucked it in her pocket for Rebekah.

The housekeeper, Frau Strobel, saw her put something in her pocket and seizing Miriam by the wrist, she'd marched her to the drawing room.

'I caught this thieving Jew taking something from your room, gnädige Frau — '

'Frau Strobel! I will not have name-calling in this house. Let the girl go so she can explain.'

Miriam's cheeks were crimson with

the shame of being accused of stealing.

'I only took this for my little sister, gnädige Frau. I know you'd finished with the magazine . . . ' She took the folded paper from her pocket and held it out for her mistress to see.

'Frau Strobel?' Frau Wachtler said, turning to the housekeeper and waiting for an explanation.

'I . . . I beg your pardon, I could've sworn she was stealing from you.'

'Apparently not. Now, if you have no further accusations, I suggest you apologise to Miriam.'

It was obvious from the housekeeper's scowl she would rather not, but she had no choice with Frau Wachtler waiting to hear her apology. However, from then on, Miriam knew Frau Strobel was waiting for an opportunity to discredit her.

Miriam hadn't told Rebekah about the incident — nor Sister Margarete who'd put so much effort into procuring the position at the Wachtlers' house. So many of the people she'd approached had not wanted to employ a Jewish girl but Frau Wachtler had agreed to take her on a trial period. She'd also been persuaded by Sister Margarete, who had suggested that as well as working as a maid, Miriam should give piano lessons to Frau Wachtler's seven-year-old daughter, Brunhilde.

It had been Rebekah who told Sister Margarete that Miriam was a talented pianist, and it had been enough to persuade Frau Wachtler that she could not only do her Christian duty and give employment to an orphan, but she could also benefit by having free lessons for her daughter.

At first, Miriam had been thrilled at the thought of being allowed to play the piano, but other than to demonstrate very simple pieces to her pupil, she was not allowed to play what she liked. It might have been worthwhile if Brunhilde wanted to learn how to play, but she had no interest at all. To make matters even worse, the other maids resented Miriam being excused work to listen to Brunhilde practise her scales. What should have been a pleasure rapidly turned into a trial.

The last thing Miriam wanted to do was cause problems for Sister Margarete, for whom she had enormous respect. The difference between life in Eichestraße and St Josef's was so great, Miriam could scarcely believe that the two places could both exist in the same city.

From the plenteous supply of delicious food freely available in her parents' house to the stews which relied on meatless bones for flavour that were served in the orphanage, from her own spacious bedroom to the shared beds crammed into the attic rooms, it was as if the two places were in different worlds.

And yet, despite the poverty at St Josef's, Sister Margarete worked tirelessly and single-handedly to feed, clothe and provide a nurturing environment for her charges. Somehow, she seemed to find time every day for each child, often with one in her arms, one on her hip and one clinging to her apron.

Miriam noticed the dark smudges

under Sister Margarete's eyes and the way that every so often, she closed her eyes briefly and sighed as though she longed for some rest. The least Miriam could do was to spare her more worry.

The previous day, while Miriam was at work, a new boy had arrived and the reaction of one of the other children at dinner had caused a row. Heinrich Redler, the eldest boy in the home, had joined the Hitler Youth and there had been regular arguments between him and Sister Margarete, especially concerning Miriam and Rebekah.

'Another Jew?' he'd asked, glaring at the new boy. 'We'll soon be overrun with them! They're spreading like sewer rats! It was bad enough having *those*,' he said, pointing at the two girls one evening as they sat down for dinner.

'Enough!' Sister Margarete handed the baby she was holding to a girl beside her and stood up.

It was so rare for her to raise her voice that everyone stopped, their spoons mid-air, waiting to see what she'd do next.

Even Heinrich was taken aback, his newly-acquired bravado deserting him.

Gripping the table, the nun leaned towards him, her large cross dangling over her soup bowl.

'You will never express such sentiments in this place again! I can't control what you do outside, nor with whom you mix, but while you're under my roof, I expect you to respect everyone I have in my care. If you feel you cannot do that, you are free to leave. Is that understood?'

Heinrich stood silent, eyes shining in defiance.

'Is that understood?' Sister Margarete repeated.

Heinrich's younger brother, Thomas, stood up.

'Please, Heinz . . . ' He tugged at the older boy's sleeve. 'Please say yes.'

Heinrich ruffled the small boy's hair. 'Yes,' he said, but it had obviously been a struggle to force the word out and he didn't look at Sister Margarete as he said it. Gently pushing Thomas back to his seat, Heinrich turned and walked out.

Sister Margarete apologised to the new boy but after a few attempts to get the children to chat as they usually did while they ate, she gave up. The meal carried on in silence, punctuated only by the sound of Thomas' snivels.

'Why does Heinrich hate us so much?' Rebekah asked Miriam when they were in bed.

'Because we're Jewish.'

'But we've never hurt him.'

'I know, Liebling. I don't understand it myself.'

'D'you think Heinrich will leave St Josef's? I wish he would.'

'I don't think so, not while Thomas is here. For such a bully, Heinrich is very caring of his brother. I don't think he'd leave him here on his own.'

'I like Thomas. He's so nice. How can two brothers be so different, Mirrie?'

'I don't know, Bekah. I felt so sorry for the new boy. What a dreadful welcome to St Josef's.'

'Can you remember his name, Mirrie? I was so shocked by Heinrich, I forgot what Sister Margarete said when she brought him in.'

'Karl Lindemann.'

'He has such sad eyes, Mirrie.'

'I know, Liebling. Sister Margarete told me while we were washing up, he's only just lost his mother. His father died . . . ' Miriam paused and added, 'some time ago.'

It was best not to tell Rebekah everything Sister Margarete had confided in her and to remind her of their own loss. In fact, Karl's father had been acquainted with Vater and he had also died in the explosion at Uncle Jacob's birthday celebration. Karl's mother had felt unwell that evening and had not accompanied Karl's father to the banquet.

Shortly after learning about her husband's death, she'd had a stroke. Karl had not left her bedside until she'd died a few days ago.

Karl, Rebekah and Miriam were drawn together by their shared religion and they became closer as reports increased of anti-Semitic attacks throughout Germany. Karl

41

always accompanied Rebekah in the morning and afternoon as they went to school. He was fourteen and in a year's time, he'd be expected to go out to work.

On several occasions when Rebekah had felt unwell and stayed off school, Karl had been waiting for Miriam outside the Wachtlers' house when she finished work in the evening.

When they were alone, they talked about their parents, life before the tragic explosion and their hopes that family or friends might be found who would offer them a home. As well as her parents, Miriam had lost several family members at the Königskrone Klub that terrible night, as well as some good family friends who would otherwise have taken her and Rebekah in.

Karl, too, had lost cousins and an aunt.

Miriam told Karl about the letters she'd sent to Boston to try to find Uncle Reuben, none of which, so far, had drawn a response, and her fears that he may no longer live in the same house — or even the same city. Karl, too, had sent letters to his father's solicitor but not received a reply.

'Could we go and visit your father's solicitor?' she asked Karl one evening. 'Surely he wouldn't turn you away.'

'He lives in London. My parents moved there when I was five. We were due to leave Cologne the morning after Herr Littauer's birthday dinner at the Königskrone Klub. If Vater hadn't left Mutter when she was sick, we'd be back in London now . . . ' He tailed off sadly.

'Can you speak English?' Miriam asked to take his mind off what might have been.

'Yes, I was young enough to pick it up easily.'

Miriam realised she was dawdling to make the journey last longer. How lovely it was to talk to Karl. She loved Rebekah and tried hard to shield her from any unpleasantness but sometimes, she wished she had someone of a similar age to confide in. Karl seemed to be matching her speed as if he, too, was reluctant to arrive.

'When I get back to London, I'll ask one of Vater's friends who works in the government if he can find your Uncle Reuben for you,' Karl said.

Her heart lurched. *When he got back to London.* She couldn't bear to think of him leaving . . . and to go so far away. With surprise, she realised how much she'd come to rely on him and to enjoy his company.

Yet he was fourteen years old — a year younger than she — and as soon as he reached fifteen, he'd have to start work at one of the nearby mines. He was tall for his age and obviously well educated, not the sort of boy who belonged underground. Yes — it was better if he could find someone who would look after him in London.

'Perhaps we could write to the town hall in Boston and see if they know your uncle,' Karl suggested, taking her silence as an indication of despair at her own circumstances.

'Do you think they have a town hall?'

'I've no idea but you could try.'

She shook her head sadly. 'I don't have any more money for stamps.'

She told Karl about Mutter's jewellery and how it had been removed from her suitcase at the police station, all except the single pearl earring.

'I sold it to a jeweller so that I'd have some money for stamps. He told me it wasn't worth very much. I'm sure he was lying but I needed the money, so I let him have it.

'It was the last thing of Mutter's I had. I don't have anything left now . . . except memories.'

Karl stopped and took her hand.

'On Sunday, when Sister Margarete takes the others to church, let's go to Königstrße.'

'What for?' She was as surprised by his suggestion as she was by him taking her hand.

'To say goodbye. Your parents and my father didn't have a funeral and if my mother did, no one told me. Just after she passed away, I was removed from our hotel room and taken to St

Josef's. But if you, Rebekah and I go to the site of the Königskrone Klub, we can say the Kaddish prayer for all our parents.'

At first, she was struck with horror at the thought of seeing the rubble and ruins of Uncle Jacob's club — the site of her parents' death — but the more she thought about it, the more she realised it would give them all a chance to close that part of their lives.

'We can find some stones to lay there,' she said. 'It's not the same as placing them on a headstone like people usually do to show their respect and love, but it'll be the next best thing.'

'Yes, that's a good idea. Shall we go and tell Rebekah?'

Miriam nodded but neither of them hurried back to the orphanage, and Karl still held on to her hand as they walked slowly along the road. It was warm and comforting and, she realised with surprise, the thought of their hands joined together made her heart skip a beat.

* ★ ★

As soon as Sister Margarete and her children had left for church, Karl, Rebekah and Miriam put on their coats and headed towards Königstraße.

It had rained during the early hours of Sunday morning, so the pavements were still shiny, and wide puddles lay in the gutter. However the clouds had sailed away and the sky was blue by the time they set out.

'D'you think we'll make it there and back before the others return from church?' Miriam asked, looking at the map Karl was holding. It looked like such a long way between where his thumb marked St-Josef-Straße and where his finger lay, above the snaking line marked König-straße.

'If we're quick,' he said.

They hadn't told Sister Margarete of their plan. It wasn't that they thought she would disapprove — quite the oppo-site — but it was something they'd planned on their own and wanted to keep private.

47

However, they knew she would expect them to be there when she returned and would worry if she didn't know where they were.

Rebekah found it hard to keep up and as they approached the business district, Miriam was relieved that the effort of trying not to fall behind meant that she didn't notice the signs in many premises and shops: *Jews Not Welcome Here*.

Once in Königstraße, Miriam began to recognise shops and buildings and knew that Uncle Jacob's club had once stood further along on the right. They walked in silence, each clutching a stone from the small garden at the back of St Josef's. Rebekah had also brought a few daisies and had defended her idea when Miriam told her it wasn't the Jewish way to place flowers on a grave.

'We place stones on headstones to show our respect.'

'I know and I've got a pretty stone, but I also like the idea of leaving flowers. I'm going to do both. I'm sure

Mutter and Vater would be pleased,' she said defiantly.

Miriam was slightly annoyed that Rebekah insisted on the flowers. It was so uncharacteristic of her sister to make up her mind about something and then take a stand on it.

Perhaps this is a good thing? Perhaps it means she's growing up at last, Miriam thought.

They reached the burned-out building which had once housed the König-skrone Klub. Standing on the other side of the street so they could take in the immensity of the destruction before them, they simply stared. The explosion had been enormous and the blaze so intense that very little of the elegant building remained, except for a few charred and blackened beams which jutted out of the huge piles of rubble towards the sky. Corrugated iron sheets had been nailed up to keep people out of the debris and Miriam gasped when she saw the hateful anti-Jewish message someone had scrawled on one of them.

How could people be so callous — so wicked?

A breath of wind blew along the street, raising dust and ashes from the ruins. Like a ghostly veil, they hung in the air, then drifted back to earth leaving a lingering aroma of burned wood.

The buildings on either side of the club were still standing. They were blackened and damaged but work had obviously been carried out to make them safe and to begin renovations.

'I heard the firefighters made more effort to stop the fire spreading than they did to actually put it out in the Königskrone Klub,' Karl said, balling his fists in anger.

A man came out of one of the apartment buildings with a broom and started sweeping the pavement. Spotting the three young people staring at the ruins, he shouted, 'What are you lot gawping at? Be off! This is a nice neighbourhood. Well, it is now the Jews have gone.' He looked pointedly at the remains of the club.

Miriam caught Karl's wrist and pulled him away.

'Please, Karl, let's do what we came to do. If you say anything or . . . ' she looked at his balled fists, ' . . . or if you do anything . . . he'll just call the police and we won't be able to say the Kaddish or leave our stones. Please.'

Karl took his eyes off the man who now had his back to them as he swept. Looking into Miriam's face, he swallowed and fought back his anger. She drew him across the road away from the man and saw with relief that he'd finished sweeping and had gone back inside the building.

'Please, Karl, we don't have much longer if we're going to be back before Sister Margarete . . . '

He nodded and she was grateful to see his jaw relax and the tension in his body melt away.

'Yes,' he said, 'let's make our parents proud.'

★   ★   ★

51

They made it back to St Josef's with just minutes to spare and were busy setting the table for lunch when the others returned from church.

'You're very quiet, Miriam. Is everything all right?' Sister Margarete asked when they were washing the dishes after the meal.

Miriam assured her she was fine. It was true. Having been able to say a final goodbye to Mutter and Vater had eased some of the pain.

All three of them had cried once the prayer had been said. They'd thrown the stones over the corrugated iron on to the charred remains of the building. It had seemed a strange thing to do but as Karl pointed out, if they left the stones on the pavement, they would only be swept or kicked out of the way. Throwing them into what was left of the building meant the stones would always be part of it — even when it was finally cleared.

Unfortunately, the man who'd shouted at them earlier must have seen Karl throw his stone, and assumed they were merely trying to cause damage. He appeared at the door, broom raised, just as the girls' stones were airborne.

'Hey! You! I've already warned you! Now get out of here! There's enough of a mess without you vandalising it. Go on! Be off with you or I'll telephone the police.'

Rebekah hastily dropped her daisies on the pavement and taking the girls' hands, Karl ran with them, down the road away from the man. They slowed as soon as he was out of sight but Karl still held on to them both until they stopped running. Then Rebekah wanted to put her gloves on. When Miriam felt his hand move in hers, she thought with disappointment that he intended to let go of hers too but he simply shifted position and interlaced his fingers with hers in the way she had seen Mutter and Vater hold hands.

Like lovers, she thought with a thrill, and then blushed. He didn't let his fingers slip from hers until they turned the corner into St-Josef-Straße and before he did, he surreptitiously raised her hand and brushed it softly with his lips.

That night, as she drifted off to sleep, she thought back over the day. She was exhausted, but it was more emotional tiredness. She still felt numb when she thought of her parents but at least she and Rebekah had paid their respects and shown their love for them today. Something inside had, at last, been put to rest.

But she was angry with herself. It was the closest she would come to a funeral for her parents and not a day to be thinking of Karl, but she couldn't put out of her mind the feeling which had rippled through her when Karl had kissed her. She chid herself for even thinking the word *kiss*.

He'd merely touched her fingers with his lips.

But wasn't that what a kiss was?

You should be thinking about your parents, she told herself and then made herself recite the Kaddish prayer in her mind before she fell asleep.

★   ★   ★

As the days went by Miriam became more certain that she and Karl had a special bond. Exactly what it was, she didn't know. Neither did she know how he felt about her, but they both recognised that it must remain hidden. Neither could guess what Sister Margarete would do if she knew how attached they'd become to each other. Would she keep them apart? Would she send one away to another home?

They were aware that their time together was limited anyway. In a few months, Karl would turn fifteen and be required to become a miner, unless someone could be found among his parents' friends who would pay for him to go to London and offer him a home.

Miriam felt sick at the thought of losing Karl, so she closed her mind to the possibility, and lived for each moment when they were alone.

There were not many. Rebekah treated Karl like an adored elder brother which meant that she constantly wanted his attention. Whenever Miriam and Karl were together, they were always accompanied by other children or Sister Margarete. Each morning and afternoon, Karl escorted Rebekah to and from school. But now, after taking Rebekah home, he immediately walked to the Wachtlers' house and waited around the corner to accompany Miriam home from work. He often arrived in time to hear the piano lessons taking place but increasingly, he heard Miriam playing a mournful solo, rather than Brunhilde Wachtler practising her scales.

'She doesn't want to play the piano,' Miriam said when he remarked on it. 'Sometimes I have to search the house for her and then when she does come, she doesn't pay attention.'

'I can hear that from the dreadful sounds she makes,' Karl said, 'but your playing . . . well, that's just wonderful!'

'I shouldn't really play the piano but it seems silly to sit there and do nothing while I'm waiting for Brunhilde to come. And it's so marvellous to play. I close my eyes and pretend I'm home with Mutter and Vater.'

'When I get to London . . . ' he said and her heart sank, 'I'll find the money to get you and Rebekah to England too. And then you'll be able to play whenever you want.'

'You will?'

'Of course! I wouldn't leave you here. And you'll love London. I'll take you to see so many wonderful things. We'll go to Buckingham Palace and Trafalgar Square.'

'But how can we see such things? Surely, we won't be allowed to visit them? We're not even allowed in a restaurant or a park in Germany.'

'England isn't like that. Nobody cares if you're Jewish. We'll be able to go anywhere we like and the place I want to take you to most of all is the Royal Albert Hall. You'll adore it. I promise you! I'll get tickets for a concert and we'll sit in a box and . . . oh, it'll be wonderful!'

After that, each evening when Karl met Miriam after work, they talked about London and planned what they'd do together. One evening, totally absorbed by their dreams of a new life together, they didn't notice that Heinrich Redler and two of his Hitler Youth friends were tailing them.

★　★　★

The following day dawned bright and clear, giving no warning of the misfortune to come.

Miriam carried out her duties in the morning at the Wachtlers' house and at three o'clock, went to the music room as usual for her piano lesson with Brunhilde. Frau Strobel had been particularly critical during the morning, and Miriam was glad of some respite, even if her pupil had not arrived.

She sat at the piano and played a

short piece Karl had said he liked. Of course, he wouldn't be outside to hear it yet but soon, he would come to walk her home. In the meantime, she would practise until she was perfect.

How wonderful it would be to explore London with him! She glanced at the clock and realised it was quarter past three. Brunhilde still had not arrived and Frau Wachtler wouldn't be happy if she found Miriam on her own at the piano. She'd found her there before and although it was obvious her daughter had no wish to learn, she refused to believe it, insisting that Miriam should try harder to engage her daughter's interest.

'She loses track of time. You must find her and teach her,' Frau Wachtler told Miriam.

She's spoilt and wilful and doesn't want to learn, Miriam thought. Still, she would be held accountable if the girl didn't turn up for at least part of the lesson.

Brunhilde was nowhere to be found in the house and when Miriam returned to the music room to see if she'd finally appeared, she was dismayed to see her mistress and the housekeeper standing by the piano, inspecting the keyboard. Frau Strobel was holding a wet cloth.

'Where is my daughter?' asked Frau Wachtler.

'I'm sorry, I can't find her, gnädige Frau, I've looked everywhere . . . '

'Were you playing the piano earlier?'

'Y . . . yes, gnädige Frau, I played a little piece while I was waiting for Fräulein Brunhilde.'

'Haven't I told you not to take liberties? The piano is not yours to play as you wish.'

'I'm sorry, gnädige Frau.' Miriam hung her head.

'You can obviously not be trusted! Such carelessness! To spill water on the keys like that!' said Frau Wachtler angrily.

'Water?'

'Yes, water! I hope nothing is damaged. What were you thinking? Drinking and eating is permitted only in the kitchen. What made you think you were an exception? I gave you special privileges but you have abused my trust. Hasn't she, Frau Strobel?'

The housekeeper nodded vigorously.

'You warned me she was trouble some time ago, Frau Strobel, but I thought it my Christian duty to give her a chance. I fear you were correct.'

'Gnädige Frau! I didn't bring water in here, I wouldn't! I swear!' said Miriam.

'The word of a Jew ... ' Frau Strobel, her arms crossed over her chest, left the sentence hanging.

'Then where do you suppose this water came from?' Frau Wachtler pointed at the wet cloth Frau Strobel held aloft. 'Such lies! Consider yourself dismissed, Miriam. I shall write to Sister Margarete in due course and inform her of your negligence and dishonesty. I no longer require the services of a girl I cannot trust. And to think I left you in charge of my darling daughter ... '

Miriam put on her coat and left. She waited until the time she and Karl usually met, then a further half hour.

Finally, she decided he must have been held up and set off.

About half way home, she saw someone bent double, clutching his stomach. As she ran towards him to help, she realised it was Karl. He was leaning against the park railings, his face bloody and swollen.

'Karl! Karl! What happened?' she cried out.

'Heinrich Redner,' he whispered as a trickle of blood ran out of his mouth and down his chin.

* * *

Sister Margarete screamed when she saw him but soon had the children boiling water, and fetching cloths and iodine to clean his cuts.

'Are you sure you didn't see who did this?' she asked several times. Karl shook his head, his eyes seeking out Heinrich's brother, Thomas.

The nun intercepted his gaze and nodded.

'I see,' she said. Miriam knew she understood that Karl didn't want Thomas to know what the elder brother he idolised had done.

When Karl's cuts and bruises had been cleaned and dressed, Sister Margarete gave him a small glass of brandy and sent him to bed.

'What a terrible day,' she said and Miriam suddenly remembered she had more bad news.

'Don't worry, child. Karl will recover soon,' Sister Margarete said, misinterpreting her stricken expression. 'There's no lasting damage as far as I can see. He'll be as right as rain in a few days. But I think we must consider how to keep you, Rebekah and Karl safe. I've been making enquiries and there may be places for you and your sister in the countryside, near Amsterdam.'

'Amsterdam?'

'I know it's a long way from here but things are getting worse. It's best to keep this from Rebekah, but attacks on Jews in Germany are increasing. The sooner you leave, the better for you and also probably for the other children here. Your presence may make them targets. I can't promise that any of the other boys won't become like Heinrich when they are of an age to join Hitler Youth. There is so much hatred being sown.'

'What about Karl?' Miriam asked. 'Can he come to Amsterdam?'

'No, the place I am thinking of is a home for girls, but I don't think there's any need to worry about Karl. I've had a reply from an English friend of mine and she's going to inform Herr Lindemann's solicitor in London about the situation. I'm sure that as soon as he hears, he'll write. With any luck, Karl will be in London very soon.

'And until I sort out places for you in Holland, I suggest Rebekah does not return to school and regrettably, you must leave your post with Frau Wachtler. I'm so sorry, child. Are you very disappointed?'

'Oh no, Sister Margarete, not at all but I think you may be with me. Frau Wachtler dismissed me today. I didn't do anything, I swear. But the house-keeper said I'd damaged the piano.'

Sister Margarete sighed.

'It's time for you all to go. I fear I cannot protect any of you for much longer.'

★   ★   ★

Miriam, Karl and Rebekah stayed at home with Sister Margarete and during the summer holidays, they were joined by the other school-aged children. Two new babies arrived at the orphanage, creating more work than ever.

Karl found a few tools in the garden shed and attempted to repair some of the broken things in the house. Miriam and Rebekah helped wash, clean and mind the younger children but occasion-ally, Miriam found herself alone with Karl for a few minutes. He would wrap his arms around her and hold her tightly until they heard the approach of some-one, then they would spring apart and carry on with what they'd been doing.

On the morning of Miriam's sixteenth birthday in October, Karl gave her a bunch of flowers and an envelope.

'It's not much. But when we're in London and I'm earning, I'll buy you a real present,' he said.

She opened the envelope and took out several sheets of paper, on which piano keys had been painted. He showed her how to place them side by side to make what looked like a piano keyboard.

'I thought you could practise playing. I know it won't make a sound but your fingers will remember which keys to touch.'

'Play it, Miriam!' said Thomas, who'd become very attached to her. 'I bet you can play it!'

They'd all laughed as Miriam sang the notes as she pretended to play. The piano game became a great favourite with the children as Miriam sang the piano notes as she 'played' a song and the children sang the words.

One evening Thomas sat on her knee and asked her to show him which keys to press to play a simple tune. Heinrich entered the room.

'Heinz!' Thomas squealed with delight. 'Heinz, you're back! How was camp?' he asked and wriggled off her knees to run to greet his brother.

Since Heinrich had started at the mine near Essen, he'd only been back to the orphanage to sleep and had often failed to do that, obviously making his own arrangements.

Sister Margarete had ensured his bed was near the door and furthest from Karl's in the boys' dormitory in the attic, ostensibly to make it easy for him when he returned late at night but Miriam suspected it was more so that he would not have an excuse to accidentally kick Karl's bed as he passed . . . or worse.

He hadn't appeared at a meal for many weeks and Miriam was shocked to see how much he'd grown. He was not only much taller but broader, and the muscles of his arms and chest strained at the tan shirt of his Hitler Youth uniform. He seemed to fill the doorframe and his appearance was so menacing that even Sister Margarete spoke with a new wariness when she asked him if he'd join them at the table for some food.

'Come and eat, Heinz! Look, we're playing the piano game and Miriam's playing for us. She was teaching me a tune when you came in . . . ' Thomas paused uncertainly as he caught sight of his brother's expression.

'We do not mix with Jews, Thomas,' Heinrich said and gently pushed his brother through the door. 'Now, go and fetch your things. Be quick! I have somewhere for us to stay.'

Thomas's eyes lit up. 'Really, Heinz? Really, we can be together?' he suddenly paused and looked back at Sister Margarete and the other children, 'Can I say goodbye first?'

Heinrich shook his head. 'This place isn't suitable for you, Thomas. I won't have you contaminated a moment longer by such filth.'

'Fil — ?' Thomas said with a frown.

'I said go!' Heinrich bellowed and the

small boy turned and ran up the wooden stairs.

Sister Margarete approached Heinrich.

'It wouldn't hurt to let him say good-bye,' she said gently. 'Remember, he was just a baby when he first came here. He knows no other life.'

'Then it's about time he did. You shouldn't be exposing him to such vile people. He must see them for what they are — cockroaches which need to be crushed.' He pounded his fist into his other hand.

'Heinrich . . . ' Sister Margarete said gently, trying to placate him but he pushed past her and walked towards Miriam with an expression of contempt on his face.

'So, you think it funny to teach my brother how to play on paper?'

'We were just having fun,' Miriam said. 'It's just a game. There's no harm in it.'

'You Jews always mean harm. The world won't be right until you've all been wiped out.'

Rebekah gasped and Heinrich turned

towards her, pushing his face towards hers.

'You said something?' Heinrich asked slowly through clenched teeth.

Rebekah shook her head, drawing back.

'That's enough,' said Sister Margarete. 'If you won't allow Thomas to say good-bye, then just go!'

Miriam saw Karl poised ready to spring but before he could act, Thomas appeared with a small bag. 'I'm ready,' he said, his gaze swinging from side to side as if trying to work out what had gone on in his absence.

Miriam held her breath. With any luck, Heinrich would simply walk out with his brother and be gone. Certainly, his expression softened at the appearance of the small boy but in a last gesture of malice, he swept his arm across the table, flinging plates and cutlery towards Miriam and Rebekah who was sitting next to her. Then, as they leapt backwards, he grabbed several of the piano sheets, frenziedly tore them into strips and screwing them into a ball, he hurled it at the fire.

'Heinz?' Thomas said uncertainly. 'Why — ?'

Heinrich took him by the arm and marched out of the room. The front door slammed.

Sister Margarete was the first to speak.

'I don't believe we shall see any more of Heinrich Redler. Sadly, I don't think we'll see Thomas again either. Such hatred! Such potential for violence! But thanks be to God, no one was hurt.' She gripped the large cross which hung round her neck with trembling fingers.

Karl had gone white and Miriam could see a vein pulsing in his temple. Knowing him as she did, she guessed it was likely he was appalled with himself for not challenging Heinrich.

'You couldn't have done anything,' she whispered to him as Sister Margarete organised the children to clear up the mess. 'And if you had, people might have got hurt.'

But he didn't reply. It was as if he couldn't meet her gaze.

'Will you make another piano, Karl?' Rebekah asked.

Karl swallowed. 'No, Bekah,' he said and ruffled her hair. 'I used up all the paint. And I don't have any more paper. But I'll make your sister something more lasting for her birthday. I won't let Heinrich spoil things for her.'

* * *

Despite Sister Margarete's certainty that Heinrich Redler would not reappear at St Josef's, she took every precaution to prevent him entering the orphanage again. No one was allowed to open the front door other than her and she asked Karl to fit a chain to it, so that she could open the door a little before admitting anyone. If Heinrich returned with a band of Hitler Youth friends, a small chain wouldn't stop them but at least she felt she was taking precautions.

She also stood at the window rocking fretful babies and looking out at St-Josef-Straße, rather than sit in her rocking chair by the fire.

After a week without incident, she started to relax. Perhaps Heinrich wasn't as vindictive as she'd believed. However, when a tall man in a suit knocked at the door, she wondered if perhaps Heinrich was craftier than she'd assumed. Herr Tischler raised his hat as he introduced himself as a representative of the Education Board.

'May I come in, please? I have some concerns.'

Feeling the tension in Sister Margarete's body, the baby she was holding began to howl as she led Herr Tischler into the kitchen.

He sat at the table and removed papers from his case and spread them before him.

'As you know, the members of the Board of Education are concerned that each child should receive an education which will equip them for work which will ultimately enrich and strengthen the Fatherland. I have been sent to review the children in your care and make sure suitable provision is being made for them.'

'I see, Herr Tischler. Well, I can ensure you that each child is suitably provided for.'

'Excellent. Unfortunately, I cannot simply take your word for it. I am required by the board to interview each child to ascertain their progress.'

'But most of the children are at school at the moment. Perhaps you'd like to return on another occasion when they're here?'

'No need, Sister Margarete. I visited the school this morning and have already seen all the children who currently reside at St Josef's. No, it is the children who are not at school today that I wish to see.' He ran his finger down a list, 'I believe there are four infants living in this orphanage who are not yet of school age and three others . . . who are. Now, let me see . . . yes . . . Karl Lindemann and Rebekah Rosenberg. Where are they and why are they not at school?'

'They're both sick.' Sister Margarete clutched the large cross which hung around her neck.

'Are they in hospital? I have no record of them being admitted.'

'No, but they've been unwell on and off . . .'

'For weeks?' Herr Tischler said running his finger down another list of figures. 'I see they both stopped attending school on the same day. Are you telling me they both came down with the same illness at the same time?'

Sister Margarete was silent.

'I would like to see both children, please. Now. And there is another child not accounted for. A Miriam Rosenberg. I understand her employment by Herr and Frau Wachtler was terminated some time ago. Has she found a new job?'

'No, not yet.'

'Well, undoubtedly, the girl will tell me herself what efforts she has made to find work.'

Sister Margarete rose slowly. There was nothing for it; Herr Tischler was determined.

By chance, Rebekah had a throat infection and answered with a very husky voice, giving credence to the story that she was unwell, but Karl had been in the garden shed cleaning a latch before he refitted it to the back door and appeared fit and healthy.

'And this young man is still only fourteen?'

'Yes, he's very tall for his age,' said Sister Margarete, 'but see for yourself, here are his papers.' She slid Karl's details across the table.

'Unfortunately, there is some discrepancy. My details suggest Karl is older.'

'No!' said Sister Margarete. 'Definitely not. I knew his father and I can vouch for the fact that he is fourteen.'

'Hmmm. Well, if you say so, Sister but I shall be carrying out further investigations. The Fatherland needs strong young men to work in industry and if this lad is not going to school, he might as well start work early. I shall recommend it to the board. As for the elder Fräulein Rosenberg, work will be found for her too if she does not find employment. Money is not provided for this orphanage so that children can idle their time away.'

'I assure you that all my children work hard — '

'That's as may be, Sister, but the fact remains that the Fatherland requires us all to pull our weight. Herr Hitler has decreed that Germany must increase its productivity and coal mining is paramount to his policy. The younger Fräulein Rosenberg will be expected to return to school as soon as possible and in due course, she too will work. Have I made myself clear?'

'Yes, indeed, Herr Tischler.'

'I will return in one month and I will expect to find changes have been made.'

Karl, Rebekah and Miriam were still sitting at the table when Sister Margarete returned from showing Herr Tischler out.

'I expect we owe that visit to our friend Heinrich Redler,' she said. 'We can only hope that it takes the board a while to investigate Karl's details. Now, I suggest I take Rebekah back to bed.

Perhaps you would keep an eye on the baby, Miriam, while I tuck your sister in.' As she left, she looked at Karl and nodded, but said nothing.

'What's going on?' Miriam asked.

'When I arrived, Sister Margarete recognised my surname and told me she knew my father. Apparently, he'd given money to the orphanage in the past. When she saw from my papers I was fifteen — nearly sixteen — she told me she'd change the dates to buy me more time. If I'm sent to work in the mines, it's unlikely anyone from London will be able to trace me. But if I stayed here and pretended to be younger, it gave me a chance of being rescued.'

'You're sixteen? But why didn't you tell me? Didn't you trust me?'

'Of course! I wanted to, but it's not my secret to tell. If the authorities find out what Sister Margarete did, she'll be in trouble.'

'So what are you going to do now, Karl?'

'Hope and pray. Vater's solicitors will

surely have received my letters by now. As soon as I can I'll arrange for you and Bekah to come with me.'

'But supposing Herr Tischler finds out before the letter comes?'

Karl shook his head sadly. 'I don't know.'

'If you're sent away to work, I'll never see you again!'

'I know. Will you meet me tonight in the garden? I've oiled all the latches and nailed down the squeaky floorboards. We should be able to creep out unheard. I've made something and I may not have another chance to give it to you.'

'What time?'

'Midnight. Everyone should be asleep by then.'

★ ★ ★

Miriam lay awake long after the other girls in the dormitory. Rebekah coughed from time to time — a dry, hacking cough which woke her and several of the other girls — but eventually, the rhythm of each girl's breathing steadied and deepened.

At last, other than the scurry of mice in the eaves, everything in the attic room was quiet. Miriam's arm had gone numb but she dared not move for fear of waking her sister who lay snuggled up to her in the narrow bed, cuddling her teddy bear, Ralf.

Miriam shifted slightly and although Rebekah stirred, she didn't waken. Finally, Miriam managed to move her shoulder sufficiently to allow feeling to creep back into her arm.

Silver beams shone in through the tiny window which lit the dormitory — at least once she and Karl reached the garden, there would be light. She shivered with anticipation. What did Karl mean, he had something for her? Had he found more paper and paint to make her a new pretend piano? If so, why hadn't he just given it to her?

The bells of St Josef's Church chimed eleven and she sighed. Another hour! She couldn't wait. There was certainly no danger of her falling asleep — she was much too excited and alert — but how was she going to lie still for another hour?

Was Karl now waiting impatiently in bed for the bells to chime twelve? Suppose he fell asleep? Surely he'd manage to keep awake for another hour. Since he'd revealed his true age, things had changed for her. When she met Karl she'd believed he was two years her junior and although he'd always behaved in a more mature way than a fourteen-year-old, in her mind he was still a boy.

She'd become very attached to him. That was hardly surprising since they shared a common religion and background as well as a common enemy in the ever-increasing number of Nazis. In fact, she'd become so attached to him, she'd wondered if she might even love him. But that had been a ridiculous notion. He'd certainly shown signs of his fondness for her — holding her hand, kissing her fingers, looking at her with such intensity, it made her cheeks burn. But she'd put those things down to a young boy's attempt to mimic grown-up behaviour.

Now she knew Karl was in fact several months older than her, there had been an enormous shift in her opinion of him. He was almost a man. No longer was she the eldest of the three Jewish children in the home, who had to shoulder most responsibility — she felt she could rely on him.

She could even love him.

Her mind hesitated over the word *love* and the thought caused her to tremble, filling her with a warm glow which made her catch her breath.

Love? Could it be true?

Did he love her?

Was that why he wanted to meet her in the garden with little chance of being discovered?

One of the girls turned over and pulled the covers higher, dragging them off the child lying top-to-tail in the same bed. Wriggling towards the warmth of the blanket, the small girl snuffled and settled down again.

The bells rang out eleven-thirty.

Should she start to get dressed?

She raised her arm off Rebekah, careful not to dislodge the blankets. Moving, then pausing, moving, then pausing, she was finally able to lift her arm out from beneath the blankets and by turning slightly, she reached towards the chair next to the bed where she'd left her dress.

By eleven forty-five, she'd climbed out of bed and was about to slip her dress over her nightdress when Rebekah started coughing and sat up. Seeing Miriam at the side of the bed, she asked sleepily, 'Are you coming to bed, Mirrie?'

Miriam let the dress slip from her fingers and climbed back into bed, wanting to cry. How long would Karl wait? How much longer until midnight? She held her breath, listening . . . listening.

Often, Rebekah seemed to wake during the night and spoke, although she wasn't really awake and usually fell asleep again very quickly.

Please, please, Miriam thought, *let it be one of those times! Go back to sleep now, Liebling.*

Minutes later, Rebekah's breathing once again deepened.

The bells of St Josef's began to chime.

Miriam held her breath and slid carefully out of bed. Rebekah didn't stir.

Six, seven, eight . . . the bells chimed.

There was no time to dress. Her shoes in her hands, she crept across the floor, taking care not to knock any of the beds, hoping the noise she was making in her haste was disguised by the clanging of the bells. She lifted her coat from the hook and, carefully raising the latch as the last peal sounded, she slipped out.

Karl called to her softly when he saw the door open. It was completely dark in the hall and she was grateful that he took her hand. After the moonlight in the dormitory, her eyes had not adjusted to the blackness. Karl felt his way along the wall to the top of the stairs and then, still holding her tightly, he led her down the steps.

She winced as he raised the latch into the kitchen and pushed the door, expecting it to squeal, but it rose silently. The back door, too, usually groaned on its hinges but it made no sound as Karl eased it open and Miriam remembered that during the previous few days she'd seen him with his tool box and oil can working on all the doors.

It was a crisp night. Other than a few wispy clouds, stars glittered in the clear sky and their breath hung in the stillness.

'I thought you weren't coming,' he said.

'Rebekah woke just as I was about to leave.'

'Does she know you've gone?'

'No. She went back to sleep. I was afraid I wouldn't get away without being seen before midnight and I didn't know how long you'd wait.'

'I'd have waited all night,' he said. 'I have a feeling time's running out for us here. I wanted to give you something before everything changes.'

She shivered. His words filled her with dread.

'Don't worry,' he said. 'The letter will come from Vater's solicitor soon and then everything will be all right. As soon as I get to London, I'll send for you and Rebekah.'

'But suppose you can't. Suppose . . . '

He placed his finger on her lips. 'Shhh. It'll be all right, I promise. But until then . . . ' He put his arm around her shoulders and led her towards the garden shed. 'I've made something for you. So, when I'm not there, you won't forget me.'

He went into the shed and emerged a few seconds later holding something in his fist.

'Close your eyes. Hold out your hand,' he said.

Miriam could smell fresh paint and expected him to put a replacement pretend piano on her hand. He'd told Rebekah he didn't have enough paint to make another. He must have found some.

However, the object Karl placed in her hand was hard and small with some fabric on it.

'Open your eyes,' he said.

Moving out of the shadows, moonlight bathed her palm. A smooth, wooden heart, the size of a pocket watch, sat on her hand. A ribbon had been threaded through a hole in the top and she lifted it, allowing the heart to dangle and spin.

'It's beautiful, Karl!' she exclaimed softly.

His face lit with pride.

'Shall I tie it around your neck?'

Standing behind her, he knotted the ends of the ribbon while she held her hair up out of his way. When he'd finished, he laid it against the back of her neck. She could feel his breath on her skin as he stood there, his hands resting lightly on her shoulders, then gently, he turned her round to face him.

Miriam lifted the heart and saw that he'd painted four letters on one side — MILD.

'Mild?' she asked. 'What does that mean?'

'That's for you to work out.' He smiled mischievously. 'Have you seen the other side?'

She flipped it over and gasped. On the right-hand side, Karl had painted a line which followed the outline of the heart. Two dots, one above the other, lay to the right of the line.

'It's a bass clef!' she said. 'I'd never noticed it's like half a heart!'

On the left, he'd painted a treble clef and, in the middle, at an angle, a tiny piano keyboard.

'Karl! It's wonderful. You're so clever!'

'One day, I'll buy you a real piano,' he said. 'In the meantime, this heart is my promise to you.'

'I'll wear it always.'

'It's best if you don't show anyone for now,' he said. 'There would be too many questions.'

Miriam nodded. 'Yes, that would be best,' she agreed, holding the heart up to admire it.

He took the heart from her and slipped one finger inside the neck of her nightdress ready to lower it inside. There was no room, so Karl undid the top button of her nightdress and then the next. His fingers brushed her chest as he folded back the material so that there was room for the heart. Miriam's breath came in short, sharp gasps and she shivered as he slid his fingers under the ribbon around her neck. After raising the heart, he allowed it to slide into the front of her nightdress. The smoothness glided down over her skin and finally, it stopped between her breasts. She shivered.

'Sorry, it must be cold,' he said.

She nodded, not wanting to tell him that it was more the shock of feeling something touching her breasts, than its temperature.

'Let me warm you,' he said. Pulling her to him and opening his coat, he wrapped it around her, holding it in place with his hands on her back. They were standing so close, she could feel the length of her body against his through the thin fabric of her nightdress, the wooden heart pressed between her chest and his.

Nothing in her life had prepared her for feeling like this. How had she not known? She pressed her cheek to his and moved her hands inside his coat until they were against his back, holding him tightly. Cupping her face with his hands, he allowed his lips to gently touch hers.

Miriam could scarcely breathe. Karl looked at her questioningly. In reply, she sought his lips with hers and hesitantly at first, they shared their first kiss. Finally, he broke away.

'I've wanted to do that for so long.'

'Must we stop?' she asked.

He nodded, resting his forehead against hers.

'But why?'

'Do you know where this could lead?'

'Well, not exactly, but . . . '

'Then that's good enough reason to stop,' he said. 'I'll never hurt you, mein Herz — my heart.'

When Miriam finally got back into bed, she was so cold her teeth were chattering. Even though Rebekah was sound asleep, she stirred as she felt the coldness of her sister's body.

Miriam's skin might feel cold to the touch, but inside, she was glowing. She replayed the night's events over and over, savouring every word, every touch and, of course, the kiss. It had been like a dream — but the proof that it had taken place was the beautiful wooden heart which she'd pulled out of her nightdress and was now caressing.

The moonlight had converted the world to black and white, so the ribbon's colour hadn't been obvious but Karl had said it was her favourite colour — red. In the morning, she would be able to see. Miriam fell asleep, holding Karl's heart tightly in her fist.

* * *

'The world is going mad!' Sister Margarete said out loud as she glanced at the previous day's newspaper. Herr Braun, one of the neighbours, often gave her old copies which she read when she could. Recently, the news had been so bad, she'd saved the papers until everyone had gone to bed, reading by the light of the dying fire.

She glanced at the date — November the eighth — this newspaper was only one day old.

The front page was devoted to a report about the assassination on the previous day of Ernst vom Rath, a German diplomat who was working in Paris. A Polish-Jewish student, Herschel Grynszpan, had apparently shot him five times at close range and had been arrested for the shooting which he claimed was a protest against the deportation of his family from Germany.

The report carried veiled hints that this scandalous incident would surely encourage even more attacks on Jewish businesses, homes and synagogues. Just in case readers were in any doubt, there were several photographs of Jewish shops and homes which had been burned during the previous months — some with Hitler Youth members posing in front of the ruins. There was even a photograph of the devastated Königskrone Klub.

Once she'd finished reading, she placed the newspaper on the fire. She watched as the despicable words of admiration towards the Nazis, delight at destruction of people's lives and the barely-hidden encouragement to violence, blackened and disappeared up the chimney.

'What is the world coming to?' she said aloud. Her words echoed around the empty kitchen.

There was so much on her mind. Two of the children had measles. The finances of the orphanage were in a poor state. She'd relied heavily on benefactors such as Karl's father to supplement their meagre income but there would be no more from him, and she knew that several other people who usually assisted her would not do so again until the Jewish children under her roof were gone. Yet she would not turn children in need away, no matter what their religion.

To make matters worse, Herr Tischler from the Education Board would be back any day and it was unlikely he'd allow Karl to remain with her.

Why hadn't the English solicitor replied? Karl was a lovely boy — educated and polite. He was good with his hands and would make an excellent craftsman or perhaps even an engineer, but that wouldn't be allowed. No, he would be expected to slave as a miner . . . He wouldn't last a month. And even if he did, as a Jew, he would be victimised . . .

She eased herself out of the rocking chair and fetched writing pad and pen. All she could do was make more enquiries about getting Karl to England. His papers were lost when his mother died and the family's belongings were confiscated by the authorities, but if she could get him to the shores of England, then surely someone would find Herr Lindemann's solicitor? He would be able to get the right papers to allow Karl entry.

Sadly for the Rosenberg girls, there was no chance of them being accepted in England without the right paperwork. They would simply be sent back to Holland or wherever they'd sailed from.

What a shame the three friends would be split up. Rebekah idolised Karl like an elder brother and she'd noticed Miriam and Karl had become closer. There would be tears when they parted.

Still, they couldn't stay at St Josef's much longer. They were in danger — and so were the other children she cared for. She'd written to her contacts in Amsterdam and heard nothing. She'd write again, to everyone she could think of.

⋆　⋆　⋆

There was something menacing in the air.

Sister Margarete had sent the letters — each dropped into the letterbox with a little prayer for its safe delivery and a speedy response. As she walked back to the orphanage, she could feel something ominous in the air, like the sensation she had shortly before a storm. Men gathered on street corners, smoking and watching passers-by — some with sticks and coshes. Groups of Hitler Youth members marched along the pavements two and three abreast, as if they owned the city. Gangs of children, encouraged by the sense of lawlessness, threw stones and hurled abuse at any Jews they met on the street. Many shops which had Jewish names over the doors remained locked, and above, curtains fluttered and trembled as people peeped out of windows.

Sister Margarete gripped the large cross which hung around her neck with both hands and hurried home. If she got there soon enough, she would stop the children from going to school. Once the pent-up aggression was released and mindless violence took hold — as she was convinced it would — children would not be safe on the streets. The uneasy feeling that in allowing Karl, Miriam and Rebekah to remain with her, she was putting the other children at risk, would not leave her.

'But what else can I do?' she muttered to herself as she hastened home.

At first, the children were excited at the thought of a day off school with the prospect that the unexpected holiday might last even longer, but the older ones picked up on Sister Margarete's anxiety. Once their requests to play outside had been denied, they wanted to know the reason.

'I believe there will be trouble in Cologne today, children. It's best if we stay home until it's over.'

Most of the children were subdued — not because they understood but because something had obviously worried the usually unruffled Sister Margarete. The prospect of trouble, however, was too much for one of the older boys who climbed the garden wall and escaped.

He returned by mid-afternoon, shaken and disturbed, describing mobs of angry people rampaging through the streets, shouting anti-Jewish slogans, smashing, burning and looting as they went. Despite his earlier bravado he was obviously upset by what he'd seen and Sister Margarete chose to ignore his disobedience and spoke to him gently rather than reprimanding him.

By the time night fell, burning could be smelled on the breeze and periodically, the smashing of glass and baying of a mob could be heard in the distance. At bedtime, Sister Margarete allowed the children to stay up.

'Will they burn us down?' a girl whispered.

Sister Margarete assured her they wouldn't.

'But . . . ?' Her eyes moved to where Karl, Miriam and Rebekah sat.

'No, Greta, they are after Jewish businesses. They will not come here.'

Confident as she made her words sound, she knew it was a possibility. Eventually, the children either slept where they sat or took themselves to bed. Only the three Jewish children and Sister Margarete sat alert.

'Tomorrow,' she said, 'I'll redouble my efforts to get you out of Cologne. I've been hoping for assistance from England and Holland but after today, I must look closer to home.'

★　★　★

Kristallnacht — Crystal Night. Such a pretty name for so many brutal atrocities, thought Miriam as she gazed in horror at the newspaper which their kindly neighbour, Herr Braun, had brought in. It was the current copy and he hadn't finished reading it, but he'd rushed it in to St Josef's for Sister Margarete to see, knowing that among her charges, she had three Jewish children.

'I thought you'd like to know,' he said sadly.

Miriam saw Sister Margarete's reluctance to show the children but it wasn't as if any of them were unaware of what had happened over the previous two days in Cologne. They didn't have specific details but they were all aware of the riots. Hadn't they all been confined to the orphanage? Hadn't they all heard the explosions, the screams and the shattering of glass? Couldn't they all smell the acrid smoke? Other than the babies and two tiny children, everyone knew.

So, Sister Margarete thanked Herr Braun for the newspaper and after spreading it out on the kitchen table, she promised as soon as they'd read the details, she would return it to him.

Miriam was amazed to see that Kristallnacht hadn't just taken place in Cologne. There had been attacks on Jews throughout Germany. It had, apparently, been a national event.

'How could so many people have known to rise up at the same time?' she asked.

'It was organised,' said Sister Margarete, shaking her head in disbelief as she read the front page and examined the photographs of burning buildings and jeering crowds. 'Look, here it says the attacks were reprisals for the murder of that German diplomat in Paris several days ago.'

'Synagogues?' Rebekah asked. 'It says here synagogues were destroyed! Who would attack a place of worship?'

No one replied.

'Now, children, I expect you to clear away the breakfast things and to either read or play a quiet game. Greta, there's washing to do and Miriam, there's a pile of darning. I will be gone a while. I'm going to leave Karl in charge as he's the eldest.'

'No, he's not,' said Greta. 'Miriam and I are older than Karl.'

'Yes . . . yes . . . of course,' said Sister Margarete, 'What I meant was that he is the eldest boy.'

'Won't it be dangerous? Suppose they hurt you?' asked Rebekah, her dark eyes open wide.

'No one will harm me, my dear. There's no need to worry. People need to stop to eat and sleep sometime — even rioters. And anyway, it looks from the newspaper like there's nothing more to destroy. Now, be good and I'll be back before you know it.'

'Where is she? She's been gone hours,' Greta wailed. 'What if she's not back before dark?'

'She will be,' said Karl although Miriam could tell he wasn't convinced. 'But if she's not, I'll go and look for her.'

'You?' said Greta scornfully. 'You're just a kid. How are you going to find her?'

'I'm sure she'll be back soon,' said Miriam quickly, She'd never actually seen Karl lose his temper but she knew the signs of building anger and feared that one day, he'd be pushed too far.

Greta had nothing against Jews but she was a selfish girl and if she thought she was being treated badly, Miriam knew she'd strike back. She was now working in a factory which she hated, and if she discovered that Sister Margarete had falsified Karl's record to keep him out of work, she would . . . well, who knew?

Just then, the sound of the key in the front door lock could be heard and they rushed into the hall.

'Ah, there you are, children. I hope everyone's been good while I've been away,' Sister Margarete said. Her pinched face was white with cold.

'You've been gone so long!' said Greta. 'I was getting worried.'

'We were all worried,' said Karl.

'Some were more worried than others.' Greta pushed past him to take Sister Margarete's coat.

'Come to the fire, Sister, you look frozen. Dinner's nearly ready,' said Miriam. She could see Sister Margarete was worried. Obviously, the news was not good.

When they were seated at the table, Sister Margarete told them about the various people she'd been to see that day. But from everyone, she'd heard the same message — until other countries agreed to accept an influx of refugees from Germany, there was little hope that Karl, Miriam and Rebekah would be able to leave.

'Rest assured, your names are at the top of all the lists,' she told them. 'If in future it becomes possible for you to leave, then we will be ready.'

* * *

On the morning of November the twenty-second, Herr Braun knocked at the door of St Josef's, brandishing the newspaper.

'It's today's,' he said. 'There's something in it that will interest you.'

The children cleared the breakfast things and Sister Margarete spread the paper on the table.

'Hot off the press,' Herr Braun said, nodding at the newspaper and folding his arms in satisfaction. 'There,' he said, pointing.

'After much political pressure on the British Government, a full-scale debate took place in Parliament on November 21st concerning the plight of refugees and the government's policy. As a result of those talks, Home Secretary. Sir Samuel Hoare, has announced that

the Home Office will grant entry visas to refugees under 17 years of age, on condition that they will not become a financial burden on the British public . . . ' Sister Margarete read. She had tears in her eyes when she looked up at Miriam. 'At last! This is your means of escape. God be praised.'

★   ★   ★

Since the previous February, when Miriam and Rebekah had arrived at St Josef's, they'd both grown. Some of Miriam's clothes were too tight and although they were still too large for her younger sister, they were now packed in Rebekah's suitcase along with her teddy bear and journal. There was no one to pass clothes to Miriam, so her suitcase was now much emptier. One clasp had broken off and Sister Margarete gave her a belt to secure it.

An inspection of Rebekah's suitcase revealed one of its clasps was threatening to break as well.

Occasionally, people donated clothes or blankets to the orphanage and just after Kristallnacht, a well-wisher had left a pair of curtains and some old children's clothes on the doorstep. One of the curtains was scorched and had probably been damaged by the many fires which had blazed across Cologne but the other was perfect. They were obviously expensive and at one time, would have hung at a window in the sort of house the Rosenbergs had lived in on Eichestraße. The dark blue brocade was decorated with golden flowers and was backed with a coarse, dark grey fabric, to cover the gold threads which ran between the flowers in each row and to prevent them from being snagged.

Sister Margarete cut and altered the undamaged curtain to fit across the back door to stop draughts but there was a lot of fabric left, so she offered to make Miriam a bag with a shoulder strap. Taking her sewing machine from the cupboard, she showed Miriam how to wind the bobbin, thread the machine and feed the fabric between the plate and the presser foot.

'But I thought you said to match the thread with the colour of the fabric,' Miriam said, looking at the dark grey bobbin.

'Ah, but I have, my dear. I am going to make it so that the grey fabric is outermost. It's stronger than the blue. But there's another reason — I don't want you to stand out. A blue bag with golden flowers on it is rather obvious. Certainly until you get away from Germany, you must blend into the background and not draw attention. Trust me.'

When the bag was finished, Miriam folded the few clothes that now fitted her and placed them inside. There was still plenty of room for whatever food Sister Margarete could spare that day, to be packed inside for the journey.

On December the third, Herr Braun knocked at the door, waving the newspaper excitedly.

'The first Kindertransport trains arrived safely in Holland! See! The first boat sailed to England yesterday! Have you heard anything yet?'

Sister Margarete shook her head sadly.

November turned to December with snow and icy winds. Herr Tischler did not return and Sister Margarete wondered if he'd been informed Karl would soon be leaving the orphanage. What point would there be in making a special journey to St Josef's to insist a boy start work in the mines when he might disappear at any time? There would be so much paperwork . . .

Karl, Miriam and Rebekah stayed home and helped with the other children and when Sister Margarete caught influenza, they ran the home. Several other children succumbed to the virus, including Rebekah and there was little time for Miriam to think, nor to mark how many days had passed since she'd heard she would be allowed to go to England.

There had been little time for Karl and Miriam to be alone since the night they'd met in the garden and she longed to feel Karl hold her to him again and kiss her — or even to hold her hand — but the babies and young children needed constant attention, as well as the patients.

They'd developed a method of communicating without speaking. Karl would raise his eyebrows as if questioning something, which she knew meant 'Are you all right?' A smile and a nod gave the answer without anyone knowing an exchange had taken place. When she briefly cupped her hand over the wooden heart which hung beneath her dress, he knew she was reminding him she was still wearing it. He would casually repeat the gesture to let her know she was his heart and sometimes, if he thought no one was looking, he would mouth the words *mein Herz* — my heart.

Finally Sister Margarete, Rebekah and the others recovered from the influenza and there were no further outbreaks. But still they heard nothing about their places on the Kindertransport train to Holland.

Christmas came and went; 1939 began.

Herr Braun still hurried in to St Josef's with the newspaper whenever there was any news about the exodus of Jewish children from Germany to England, keen to know if they'd received a call for Miriam, Rebekah and Karl. Clothes no longer remained packed. They were taken out as necessary and every night Ralf the bear joined Rebekah in bed. But each morning, whatever wasn't being worn or used was re-packed.

Despite still being weak after her illness, Sister Margarete braved the ice and snow to walk to the Jewish Council who'd promised to secure places to England for the three young people, to enquire how much longer it would take. She returned subdued. There were so many children whose parents had applied for them to leave that the lady she'd spoken to said they'd been inundated but they were working as fast as they could.

'Be ready for immediate departure,' the woman had said. But, as Karl observed, she'd said that in November when Sister Margarete had first put their names down.

At last, five days into the new year, Sister Margarete received tickets for the Kindertransport train leaving Cologne the following day.

Everyone got up earlier next morning. Sister Margarete prepared porridge, then wrapped slices of bread and cheese in paper which Miriam put in her bag. Herr Braun also arrived early, obviously informed of their imminent departure because he did not bring a newspaper — just three British sixpence coins which he'd saved from when he'd spent time in London years before. Sister Margarete had sewn each of them a purse out of the blue curtain fabric and Greta had knitted a lopsided jacket for Rebekah's teddy.

She expected to feel nothing but relief at leaving the orphanage but as they waited in the hall for Sister Margarete to tie her green headscarf, Miriam felt tears prick her eyes.

Karl opened the door and they stepped into the grey morning. The wind was bitter, and after waving, Herr Braun went back to his house. Greta stood at the door of St Josef's with the other children, waving, but she'd closed the door before the refugees turned the corner, as if to shut them out of their lives for good. *At least now they won't be under threat because of us*, Miriam thought.

By the time they arrived at the railway station the steady drizzle had drenched them and Sister Margarete, who had not regained her strength after her illness, was shivering. Miriam tried to convince her to go home, but she wanted to see the Kindertransport train off. After asking an official for directions, she suggested they hold tightly on to each other as they squeezed through the crowds. Gripping Rebekah with one hand and her case in the other, Sister Margarete pushed her way through the throng. With her bag slung over her body, Miriam had both hands free, so she could hold on to Rebekah and Karl.

Miriam looked at the enormous station clock. They'd arrived early but it was taking a long time to fight their way through to get to Platform Two.

Around them, children sobbed and clung to parents. Others were silent, eyes wide in bewilderment. Adults smiled bravely, although their eyes brimmed with tears.

A shrill whistle pierced the air to attract attention and a railway guard began to make an announcement but his words were drowned out by the screams of a child clutching at his mother's coat. Sister Margarete, at the front of the group, suddenly increased her pace and Miriam wondered if the message concerned the Kindertransport train. Suppose they couldn't get to it in time? They would surely not be given another chance to leave.

Closer to Platform Two, the crush increased as parents carrying small children and pushing older ones forward, streamed towards the ticket barrier and then waited there to wave their children goodbye. Rebekah looked back over her shoulder towards Miriam, her gaze darting left and right at the adults who towered over her and who had eyes only for their own children. They would not notice if a small girl was lost in their midst. Miriam smiled encouragingly at her sister.

'Don't let go of Sister Margarete,' she shouted.

When they reached the ticket barrier, the guard glanced at their paperwork and pushed them on to the platform where the almost solid mass of children seemed to move as one towards the train. Miriam turned to look for Sister Margarete. There was so much she wanted to say before she left, but now there would be no chance. Who could have foreseen such chaos?

Miriam dared not let go of Karl and Rebekah — even to wave. She caught a glimpse of the small, bird-like woman with the green headscarf, whose selfless love had filled their lives for almost a year and then a large man clutching two children to his chest blocked Miriam's view.

I will write and thank you, Sister Margarete, Miriam vowed silently. She imagined her letter arriving at the orphanage and being placed on the mantelpiece next to the small stone figure of St Josef, be opened and read out during dinner.

The statuette had intrigued her. A bearded man dressed in a robe who came from another age. How much more appropriate, she thought, if the orphanage had been named St Margarete's.

★ ★ ★

Shrill whistles blew on the platform, carriage doors slammed and steam hissed from the engine, signalling the departure of the train. Older children clutched younger ones tightly, sitting rigidly in their seats and looking about the carriage as if searching for their parents. Karl found two places together and pulling Miriam next to him and Rebekah on to his knees, he put his arms protectively around both of them.

The sound of the engine whistle and the chug, chug, chug of the pistons, prompted tears from many of the children in the carriage and a few screams of terror as the train pulled out of the station — slowly at first and then gathering speed.

Those closest to the windows rubbed clear circles in the condensation on the cold glass, trying to catch sight of anything which was still familiar before it was all gone. But the clouds of steam from the engine, the children's breath and their still-wet coats filled the air with moisture which turned back to water droplets on the cold glass. The smell of smoke, steam and damp wool hung heavily in the air and Miriam knew that if she were ever to encounter such a combination of aromas again, it would remind her of this time — excitement at the thought of a new life and the security of Karl's arm around her. For the other refugees in the carriage, she wondered whether the smell would conjure up similar happy thoughts or would their memories be of fear and misery?

Miriam had no idea how long the journey would take and was surprised when the train stopped with a hiss of steam and squeal of brakes.

'Are we there?' Rebekah asked.

Karl shook his head,

'Not quite, we're stopping at the border.'

Miriam noticed he was biting his lip and had his hand on the waistband of his trousers. She knew he'd concealed a ring that once belonged to his mother there and wondered why he appeared so anxious. She knew he'd travelled this way with his parents many times; surely, he was overreacting? How could anything stop them now?

Minutes later, she knew exactly why Karl appeared so nervous. A chill blast blew into the carriage as its doors were thrown open and six soldiers entered.

'Everyone off the train!' the sergeant yelled.

The children lined up on the platform, white-faced with fear as they warily eyed the soldiers and their Alsatian dogs.

'All identification documents must be shown, all bags open for inspection,' the sergeant yelled.

'What are they looking for?' Miriam whispered.

'Anything of value. It'll be fine,' Karl muttered.

The soldiers rummaged in all the luggage, carelessly pulling out clothes and belongings lovingly packed by parents.

One soldier snatched a colourful bag from a young girl and tipping its contents onto the floor, he placed a confiscated bar of chocolate and a new doll inside, laughing to his friend that his sister would be pleased with them. Miriam silently thanked Sister Margarete for her forethought in making her bag unremarkable. But nothing of value was found in the luggage and once the soldiers had checked the papers, children scrabbled on the floor to reclaim and repack possessions.

'Will they let us go now?' Rebekah asked.

'When they've checked everyone on the train, Liebling,' Miriam said, hardly daring to breathe in case the soldiers changed their minds and carried out further searches. What would they do to Karl if they found the hidden ring?

Eventually, they were allowed back into the carriage. Doors slammed, the whistle blew, clouds of steam escaped with a hiss and the train pulled slowly away. Karl breathed a sigh of relief.

'We're in Holland! They can't stop us now! Just a few more hours and we'll be on the boat!'

When Karl's legs went to sleep under Rebekah's weight, Miriam invited her to sit on her lap.

'Put your arm around me like before, Karl,' Rebekah said as she settled on Miriam's knees.

'Bekah, it's not very comfortable for Karl to lean forward and put his arm around you.'

Rebekah jutted out her chin in the way she'd started to do during the last few weeks,

'But he still has his arm around you, Mirrie.'

'Here,' said Karl, 'I'll hold your hand instead. How's that?'

Miriam wanted to tell her sister off for being selfish but Karl's solution had satisfied her.

After several hours, during which time many of the smaller children had fallen asleep, the train slowed. The whistle blew, bells rang and brakes squealed, waking all but the most exhausted. With a hiss and shudder, the train came to a halt.

Karl, who'd been to a sea port before, said he could hear the cry of gulls overhead which surely meant they were near the sea. The windows were still steamed up and with the renewed sobbing and chatter inside the carriage and shouts from the platform, Miriam couldn't hear the sea birds and she hoped Karl was right.

A smiling woman holding a clipboard entered the carriage and after welcoming the children in heavily-accented German, she asked them all to follow her. Once on the platform, other women lined the refugees up and led them out of the station. Now, Miriam could hear the gulls wheeling overhead and taste the salt on the breeze and if any further proof were needed, she saw signs that read Hoek van Holland — Hook of Holland.

Taking Rebekah's hand, she linked arms with Karl. Soon, they would be in England and a new life would begin where they would be accepted without question and then, surely, the possibilities were endless.

'Can I go in the middle, please, Mirrie?' Rebekah asked, letting go of her hand and pulling their linked arms apart. Karl took Rebekah's hand, then smiling over the top of her head at

Miriam, he mouthed *Mein Herz* to her.

This was a new side to Rebekah which had only become evident during the last few weeks.

'A phase,' Sister Margarete had said. 'Under normal circumstances, Rebekah would be growing up and finding her own way. But the times we're living through now are anything but normal, so be gentle with her, even if she's a little demanding, Miriam. Remember, she's still a child.'

Miriam regretted the stab of annoyance she'd felt when Rebekah had pushed in between Karl and herself. Sister Margarete had been right; 'normal' had not existed for the sisters since February the previous year. She must be kinder.

Karl was always gentle with Rebekah, she thought fondly, cupping her hand over the wooden heart which the weight of her coat was holding against her chest. *That's why I love him*, she thought and a thrill ran through her.

She loved him and although he hadn't said it, she thought he loved her too.

And soon, they would be in England — together.

*   *   *

The children were taken to a large warehouse and as they filed through the door, they were each handed a mug of hot cocoa and a cake. A tear slipped down Miriam's cheek. How wonderful the Dutch people were! They smiled at the refugees as they handed out drinks and food, and even when they spoke to the children in Dutch, their kind intentions were obvious.

How different from people like Heinrich Redner and the others whose lives were filled with hatred.

Orderly queues were formed with boys on one side and girls on the other. Nurses in crisp uniforms took small groups of children into side rooms where they were given a medical.

'Suppose we don't pass? What'll happen?' Rebekah asked, her chin trembling.

'I don't know, Liebling, but I'm sure

we will,' Miriam said, watching Karl's progress in the boys' queue which seemed to be moving much faster than the girls'. Suppose Karl should be separated from them? How would she find him again?

The two sisters were taken into a side room by a nurse and once the white-coated doctor had checked their papers, they were both examined.

Surveying Miriam doubtfully over the top of his glasses, he said, 'Your pulse is elevated. Do you know if you have a heart condition?'

'No!' Miriam said in alarm, wondering if she would be allowed to go to England if the doctor thought she was unfit.

'She seems a bit agitated, doctor,' the nurse said. 'There's nothing to worry about, you know,' she added, turning to Miriam.

'Yes, yes. It's just that we're travelling with someone else and I'm so afraid we won't be able to find him,' Miriam said, hoping her explanation would persuade the doctor to stamp her paper as he'd already stamped Rebekah's.

'I see. And this person is a brother?'

Miriam was about to say 'friend' but decided there would be more chance of finding Karl if everyone thought he was a member of her family.

'Yes,' she said and hoped Rebekah would not contradict her. As the nurse took her pulse again Miriam concentrated on slowing her racing heart by imagining her and Karl strolling through the streets of London together. It seemed to work as the nurse reported that her heart had slowed.

The doctor stamped her papers and handed them to her with a smile. 'I'm sure you'll find your brother waiting for you outside. Bon voyage!'

'Thank you for not telling the doctor Karl isn't our brother, Liebling,' Miriam murmured. 'I know it's a lie but it might mean people will let us travel together if they think we're a family.'

Karl was indeed waiting for them.

'I was beginning to think they weren't going to let you through,' he said, his face lighting up with relief. He led them to one of the queues for the ferry. 'Another hour and we'll start to board.'

'An hour?' Rebekah said with a frown. 'I'm hungry. Have you got food left, Mirrie?'

'No, Liebling, we finished the bread and cheese on the train. I'm afraid you're going to have to wait. You just had cocoa and a cake . . .'

'That was ages ago,' Rebekah said and crossed her arms over her chest.

'I'm hungry too. We just have to be patient.'

'I'll go and see if I can get some more cake,' said Karl, putting his case down next to Miriam. 'They might give me some. It's worth a try.'

'No!' said Miriam. 'We ought to stay together. Rebekah will just have to wait.'

Rebekah's mouth set in a hard line.

'I'll go and ask,' said Karl. 'I won't be long.'

'Karl cares that I'm hungry,' said Rebekah.

Miriam stifled a sharp retort as Sister

126

Margarete's words came back to her — *Be gentle with her, even if she's a little demanding.*

* * *

Twenty minutes later, Karl had not returned and the queue had started to move forward as the passengers began to board the boat.

He had still not returned by the time Miriam and Rebekah reached the officials who were checking passengers' travel documents at the door out of the warehouse.

Rebekah started to sob, aware it was because of her that Karl had left them to search for food.

'I'm sorry, Mirrie, I'm so sorry!' she wailed.

'Papers?' the ticket inspector said and then noticing Rebekah's tears and Miriam's distress, added, 'Is there a problem?'

'We're waiting for . . . our brother,' Miriam said. 'He went to try to find some food.'

'I see. What's your brother's name?'

'Karl. He's taller than me, slim with dark hair.'

'Stand to one side and I'll get some-one to see if we can find him,' the man said, beckoning to a colleague. 'Pieter, can you see if you can find these young ladies' brother for me?' the man asked, tucking their papers under his arm and moving Miriam and Rebekah out of the queue.

'What's his name?' Pieter asked.

'Um, I think they said Karl. He's got dark hair.'

'Most of them have dark hair. What's his surname?' Pieter scowled. He'd been drinking coffee and taking a well-earned break when he'd been called back to hunt for a wayward boy.

The man took the papers out from under his arm and looked at Miriam and Rebekah's details. 'Rosenberg,' he said. 'The girl said he was last seen going over that way.' He pointed vaguely towards the other end of the warehouse.

Pieter walked along the queue,

cupping his hands to his mouth called for Karl Rosenberg but if the boy was in the queue, he didn't respond. Starting at the back of the second queue, Pieter worked his way forwards calling out for the boy and wondering how cold his coffee would be by the time he got back to it. He'd just got to the front of the line when a dark-haired lad stepped forward. 'I . . . I'm Kurt Rosenberg,' he said, holding out his papers. 'Did you want me?'

'Kurt?' Pieter paused for a moment. He thought the ticket inspector had said Karl but he might have been mistaken. The surname was Rosenberg, he was sure of that, so the boy must be the right one.

'Well, you should be ashamed of yourself worrying your sisters like that!' he said.

'I . . . I'm . . . '

'Move along now!' the ticket inspector said irritably and the boy gratefully hurried forward.

Pieter returned to the head of the other

129

queue where Miriam and Rebekah were still waiting. 'Their brother's just gone through the other ticket barrier,' he told the official who took the papers out from under his arm, stamped them, placed name labels around the girls' necks and gestured for them to go through the barrier.

'I have Karl's suitcase.' Miriam picked it up.

'I'll take it to him,' Pieter said, looking longingly at where he'd left his coffee.

The boy had already passed through the barrier by the time he got to the other queue, so he handed it to one of the officials going with the Kindertransport children on the boat.

'This is for Kurt Rosenberg,' Pieter said. 'He's already gone through. Can you make sure he gets it, please? Perhaps you can tell him his sisters will be boarding soon.'

Miriam had overheard the ticket inspector say the boat was to leave slightly ahead of schedule to try to beat the storm expected on the North Sea that night, but as the girls stepped out of the warehouse, it appeared the bad weather had already set in. Sleet blew almost horizontally across the port, driven by a wind that whipped away words as soon as they were uttered.

'I can't see him, Mirrie,' Rebekah shouted, clinging on to her sister's arm

'Let's get on the boat. We'll find him there,' Miriam shouted back. The man had assured her Karl would be aboard by the time they reached the top of the gangplank but until she laid eyes on him, the gnawing sensation in her stomach wouldn't go away.

Biting wind whipped their hair across their faces as they reached the bottom of the rear gangplank and started to climb. Miriam looked towards the front of the ferry to try to judge its size but it was so long, it merged into the dark and driving sleet.

How would she find Karl on such an enormous boat? He'd told her the crossing would take most of the night and with such a dreadful gale, it could take longer, so she would have plenty of time to look for him — but if he was moving about, looking for her, they might keep missing each other.

The man had assured her Karl had already boarded but it seemed odd he hadn't rejoined them in the queue — unless for some reason he'd confused the lines and, not seeing them, assumed they'd already gone through the barrier.

Or perhaps the man had been mistaken and Karl was still in the warehouse looking for them. Miriam felt sick with anguish.

★ ★ ★

'I feel sick, Mirrie,' Rebekah wailed, holding a handkerchief to her mouth.

The ferry had left the relative calm of the harbour at the Hook of Holland only ten minutes before, and now it pitched and rolled on the waves, forcing passengers to stagger drunkenly as they looked for a place to sit during the voyage.

'Lay your head on my lap, Liebling,

you'll feel better if you're lying down,' Miriam said, brushing the damp fringe off her sister's grey, clammy forehead. She glanced about for Karl, but members of the crew had encouraged passengers to remain seated and after a while, no one new came into their seating area. Judging by the lack of conversation, the white or even green faces and the moans, the motion of the boat on the rough seas was making most people queasy. Miriam leaned back and closed her eyes.

When she awoke, the winds had subsided considerably and she overheard someone say they would be docking shortly. Gently she shook Rebekah awake and stood up to stretch.

'Let's go out on deck, Liebling. If we're one of the first off, we can look at all the passengers as they pass. If Karl's aboard, we'll surely find him.'

'If?' Rebekah asked. 'You said if! That man told us he was aboard!'

'I know, Liebling, but I don't know if he made a mistake. Why would Karl have joined a different queue? He'd have come back to find us.'

Rebekah's hands flew to her mouth.

'Oh, Mirrie! D'you really think so?' She began to cry. 'It's my fault, isn't it? It's all my fault!'

Miriam knelt in front of her and put her arms around her. 'We don't know for sure he's not on the ferry, Liebling. If we go now, we can check as many people as possible.'

At the bottom of the gangplank, members of the crew directed passengers to the arrival hall, and Red Cross volunteers gathered the Kindertransport children. Miriam scoured the crowds for Karl, standing on tiptoe. Eventually, the lady from the Red Cross called out in German to the large group, instructing them to follow her.

Miriam placed a restraining hand on Rebekah's arm, preventing her from following the crowd.

'We'll just wait for a few minutes. We'll catch up easily,' she said.

One of the seamen who was directing passengers, thinking that they would get lost, pointed at the Red Cross lady who was holding her umbrella high at the front of the group. In English, he told the two sisters to follow. Miriam didn't understand the words but his intention was clear. She told him in German she had to wait for her brother but the man didn't understand her and called one of the other Red Cross volunteers to escort the two girls to the arrival hall.

It hadn't occurred to Miriam she would have problems either understanding or making herself understood in England. If Karl had been there, he'd have translated.

But then if Karl had been there, they would now be among the group who'd almost reached the arrivals hall, she thought, and a great wave of sadness washed over her. She allowed herself and Rebekah to be led away by the kind Red Cross lady who spoke a little German and explained they had to catch a train. Perhaps they would find their brother on the railway platform.

Once inside the arrival hall, the girls

were handed over to another volunteer who offered them sweet tea and biscuits.

'Welcome to England, my dears,' she said. Seeing how troubled they were, she crouched and said in halting German. 'You mustn't be upset, my dears. You're safe now. You don't need to worry any more.'

Miriam swallowed back her tears and explained that although they were grateful to have finally reached England, they were sad because they'd lost their brother.

'Drink up before it gets cold,' the woman said. 'And don't worry. I'm sure he must be here somewhere. How old is he?'

'Sixteen,' Miriam said at the same time as Rebekah said 'Fourteen.'

The lady laughed. 'Have you lost two brothers?'

'He's sixteen,' said Miriam firmly, glaring at Rebekah, 'and his name is Karl.'

'I see. And your surname?'

'Rosenberg,' said Rebekah.

The woman wrote *Karl Rosenberg* in a notebook.

'Oh no, Karl's surname is Lindemann,'

Miriam said and with a flash of inspiration, she added, 'Karl's our half-brother.'

'Oh, I see. You wait here and finish your tea and biscuits while I look for someone with a list of the children who sailed from Holland.'

She returned a few minutes later. Her lips were pressed tightly together.

'I'm so sorry, my dears, but there was no one by that name on the boat.'

'But the man told us Karl had boarded!' Rebekah said. 'He told us, didn't he, Mirrie?'

But Miriam couldn't speak.

4

'Perhaps you would care to tell me — '
the policeman looked down at the
papers on the desk in front of him and
ran his finger across the page as he read
— 'Karl Lindemann ... why you
thought it appropriate to punch one of
the people working hard to send you to
a safe haven?'

Seated on the other side of the desk,
Karl groaned and hung his head.

How could he have been so stupid?
Hadn't Miriam told him on several occasions he must learn to curb his temper?

'Look, Karl, I can see you're sorry,
but I still need an explanation.' The
policeman looked through Karl's documents. 'I can see you have been living in
an orphanage and I believe you were
travelling with two other children from
that orphanage. Is that correct?'

'Yes, sir.'

'I see, well, perhaps you'd like to tell me why you left your friends.'

Karl swallowed. 'Well, sir, Rebekah — the younger one — was hungry. Sister Margarete wasn't able to spare much food when we left. So I thought I'd ask if I could have some more cakes. The lady gave me some, wrapped in a napkin. When I tried to get back to Miriam and Rebekah, a man stopped me and said I had to have a medical test.

'I tried to get my papers out of my pocket to show him I'd already had one and he saw the cakes. He accused me of stealing. When I told him the lady gave them to me, he called me a liar and grabbed my collar. I could see the queues were moving to get on the ship and . . . well, I panicked. I couldn't bear the thought of losing Miriam and Rebekah . . . so . . . '

'You punched him,' the policeman finished.

Karl nodded and hung his head again.

'Luckily for you, the lady who gave you the cake came forward and spoke for you and I can see you have, indeed, had your medical check . . . '

The policeman paused. Karl looked up.

'Are you going to send me back to Germany?'

'No, definitely not. We're trying to help you. I understand you've come from a society where violence seems to be occurring with great regularity but you must realise we are your friends. Bringing violence with you will not help.'

Karl nodded and swallowed.

'You will be allowed to continue your journey but I'm afraid your friends sailed on the last ferry.'

Karl squeezed his eyes shut.

I am a man. I will not cry, he thought, *I will not.*

★ ★ ★

The policeman escorted Karl back to the queue of passengers waiting to board a ferry.

'Do you have any luggage?' he asked.

Karl suddenly realised he didn't have his case.

'I left it with Miriam and Rebekah.'

After checking with the ticket inspectors, he suggested that perhaps the girls had taken the case on board, rather than leave it unattended.

It made sense and Karl hoped that it was so because in the suitcase, he had a letter for Miriam in which he'd written the names and addresses of all the people he knew in London — Ridley and Perkins, his father's solicitors as well as all the friends of his parents that he could remember.

Sooner or later, she would open the case and find the envelope addressed to her. Then, it would be a simple matter for her to contact someone and hopefully, by that time, Karl would be in London. He'd planned to give the letter to her when they reached London, where he knew she and Rebekah would be sent to a hostel and then hopefully to a family. Neither of them knew where they would ultimately be living but at least she could contact him via the solicitor. He had been saving it until the last minute because also in the envelope, he'd told her what the letters on the back of her wooden heart, stood for.

MILD. Miriam, Ich Liebe Dich. Miriam, I love you. I love you with all my heart, he'd written.

He felt sure she knew how he felt but he'd never summoned the courage to actually say the words. He wondered if she'd guessed. As soon as they were reunited, he'd ask her. And he'd say the words out loud.

There was nothing in the case of any value other than the letter. He had a few clothes, but nothing that couldn't be replaced as soon as he was in London. He touched the waistband of his trousers. The only valuable thing he had on him was hidden inside it. He had no idea how much of his father's estate had been in Germany and therefore confiscated by the Nazis. They'd owned a house in Cologne which was rented out while they were living in England; he knew it had been seized, as well as all the money his father had deposited in a German bank. Everything his parents had with them in the hotel room in Cologne was also taken — except the ring, which his mother gave him shortly before her death.

After Karl's father died, his mother had suffered a stroke. The doctor said it hadn't been severe but it was as if she'd given up. Karl nursed her, staying with her night and day until one morning, she'd instructed him to bring her jewellery box from the hotel safe and taken out a ring he'd seen her wear many times. He'd assumed it was a sapphire but his mother told him it was a priceless blue diamond.

She instructed him to make a small slit in the waistband of his trousers and once the ring had been inserted, she painstakingly sewed it up. The effort had exhausted her.

'Put the rest of the jewellery back in the hotel safe, Karl. It will all be stolen but at least no one will suspect you have something worth more than the rest of the pieces put together. I hope the ring will help you escape this madness.'

The following day, she'd passed away. As she'd predicted, her jewellery and all their other belongings were taken, once the hotel manager realised she'd died and that Karl would not be able to pay for the suite.

When he got to England, he'd find out how much money his father had in London. If as he suspected it wasn't much, he'd sell the ring.

★　★　★

For Miriam, the journey on the train to Liverpool Street Station in London passed in a blur of tears. At first, she'd refused to get on. The guards, who didn't speak German, were sympathetic at first but became increasingly frustrated at the young foreign girl who didn't seem to understand if she didn't get on the train within the next few minutes, she'd be spending the night on the station.

144

Finally Rebekah persuaded her to climb aboard. The nice Red Cross lady had promised that if she came across a Karl Lindemann the next day, she'd let him know the girls were on their way to a hostel in London and give him the address.

Miriam was subdued during the journey, staring out of the window, resisting the attempts of two girls sitting opposite them in the carriage to engage them in conversation. The older girl introduced herself as Anja Marks. She appeared to be about the same age as Miriam and her sister, Kathrin, was about Rebekah's age.

'We're from Düsseldorf,' Anja said. Miriam simply nodded. 'Where are you from?'

'Are your parents still there?' Anja asked when Miriam told her they'd lived in Cologne. 'Ours are, aren't they Kathrin?' she added.

When Miriam told them they'd been living in an orphanage, Anja's round face fell.

'Oh no! I'm so sorry. Now, don't you

worry. Kathrin and I will look after you, won't we Kathrin?'

Miriam sighed. She didn't want to talk to anyone. She didn't want to think about anything. Her mind was blank. Recognising the silent plea in Rebekah's eyes, she smiled and thanked Anja.

'Can you speak any English?' Anja asked.

Miriam shook her head.

'Don't worry. We do, don't we, Kathrin? If there's anything you need translated, just ask.'

'Thank you,' said Miriam. 'I wish I'd learned English before we came.'

'We had lessons at school,' said Anja. 'Vater was going to bring us to England for a holiday so I tried really hard but . . .' She tailed off sadly. 'Well, it wasn't to be . . . Still, when Vater and Mutter can get their travel papers, they'll come for us, won't they Kathrin?'

The younger girl nodded in agreement.

When Anja and Kathrin went to find the toilet, Rebekah took the opportunity to complain about Miriam's lack of interest.

'Honestly, Mirrie! You're being so unfriendly! I think they're both really nice and they've offered to translate for us.'

Miriam was surprised at Rebekah's anger. She bit back an angry retort and after taking a deep breath, she said, 'I'm sorry, Bekah. I just feel so wretched without Karl.'

'Anyone'd think he was just *your* friend, Mirrie! He was my friend too and I miss him! Oh, by the way,' she added triumphantly, 'Karl *is* fourteen. I don't know how you could have forgotten that! He went to school with me, so I know!'

Miriam sighed. The last thing she wanted was to argue with her sister.

'Karl is sixteen, Liebling. He'll be seventeen soon. Sister Margarete changed the date of birth on his records. If the authorities had known, he would have been sent to the mines. That was why we were so worried about Herr Tischler from the Education Board coming back — '

'We? You said *we*. You knew he was sixteen and you didn't tell me?' Rebekah asked incredulously.

'It wasn't any of your business,' said Miriam, 'and the more people who knew, the more likely it was the truth would get out. Then Sister Margarete would've been in serious trouble.'

'Karl was my friend too, Mirrie.'

'I know, but he wasn't any less your friend because you didn't know his real age.'

'So how did you find out?'

'The day Herr Tischler came to St Josef's — Karl told me just after he'd left.'

'So you kept it a secret from me?'

'It wasn't my secret to tell, Liebling.'

Rebekah crossed her arms and turned away from Miriam, 'Well, I hope you're going to be nicer to Anja and Kathrin when they come back!'

'Yes, I will,' said Miriam. *Anything to avoid a fight*, she thought.

Despite herself, Miriam was drawn to the chatty Anja and her quiet sister and it would certainly be useful to have someone who understood English until she and Rebekah could fend for themselves.

'I hope we'll be placed with families who aren't too far apart,' said Anja, 'then hopefully we can meet up. As soon as I'm settled, I'll write to Mutter and Vater and tell them where we are . . . '

'S'pose they've moved out before your letter arrives?' Kathrin asked.

'I don't know. But if I write quickly, they should get it.'

Anja explained to Miriam and Rebekah that their father's clothes shop had been raided and he'd lost all the stock.

'To make matters worse,' she said, 'Vater had taken most of the money out of the bank and kept it in the safe. So, we lost almost everything. But I'm sure they'll get the right papers soon and join us in England. Oh,' Anya said, looking stricken. 'How thoughtless of me, I'm so sorry to go on about our parents, when you haven't got any,' she added, leaning forward to pat Miriam's knee. 'It must be awful.'

Miriam told them about the explosion in the Königskrone Klub and how they'd lived with Sister Margarete and the other children.

'No wonder you seem so sad,' said Anja. 'I said to Kathrin earlier that you looked really unhappy, didn't I, Kathrin?'

'We were supposed to be with someone else,' Rebekah said, 'but we don't know where he is.'

'Oh dear. A friend or a relative?'

Rebekah looked at Miriam and raised her eyebrows.

'Friend,' said Miriam quickly. She hadn't wanted to tell the girls about Karl — it was too raw and she wondered if Rebekah had realised her reluctance. But since her sister had mentioned him, Miriam thought it best to be honest. If she hadn't told the man at the ticket barrier in Holland she was looking for her brother, he wouldn't have assumed Karl and she shared a surname. And then, perhaps, he'd have found Karl.

'Friend of us both,' said Rebekah.

By the time the train arrived at Liverpool Street Station, Anja had taught Miriam and Rebekah how to tell someone their names and ages in English.

'How will we manage on our own, Mirrie?' Rebekah asked. The petulant girl had given way to the worried child Miriam was used to.

'We'll pick it up, Liebling,' Miriam said with as much confidence as she could muster.

Once the Kindertransport children got off the train, they were separated into small groups, led off the platform and out of the station. Miriam was relieved to see Anja and Kathrin were in her group and as the lady who was ticking off their names spoke to them, Anja translated.

'Her name's Mrs Cohen. She's from the Stepney Jewish Committee. She's going to take us to a hostel where some of us will be met tonight by our new families and some of us will sleep there and be met tomorrow.'

Mrs Cohen was a large, athletic woman who set off from the station at a speedy pace. She told Anja the hostel wasn't far, but after travelling so many hours from Germany, most of the children were exhausted and soon became out of breath.

'Is it much further, Mirrie?' Rebekah asked. Her cheeks were red with having to walk so fast.

'I don't know, Liebling, I've never been here.'

'Well, can't you ask her to slow down?' Rebekah asked crossly.

'Rebekah! I understand you're tired. So am I. But you know I can't ask her anything because I don't know how to say it in English!'

Miriam was trying hard not to lose her temper but she was tired and hungry and the ache she felt at losing Karl was overwhelming.

'You never call me by my full name!' Rebekah said in an accusing tone. 'Do you, *Miriam*?'

'We're both tired, Liebling,' said Miriam in the calmest voice she could summon. 'So let's not fight over each other's names.' She swapped her sister's suitcase to the other hand and shifted the strap of the bag on her shoulder, trying to ease her tired muscles.

Rebekah tossed her head but fell silent.

When they arrived at the Stepney Jewish Hostel, several couples were waiting and led away the children who were to stay with them. The rest were taken into the hostel and given large bowls of soup and chunks of bread. Rebekah ignored Miriam, choosing instead to sit next to Kathrin.

'It looks like our sisters are getting on well,' said Anja, sitting next to Miriam. 'I'm sure we're going to be the best of friends too.'

That night the remaining refugees were taken to their dormitories. There were more beds than girls, and the manager said they could choose which bed to sleep in. Miriam expected Rebekah would sleep with her as usual, but instead, her sister chose a bed next to Kathrin.

That night, for the first time in almost a year, Miriam went to bed alone. She tried to convince herself it was a good thing. After all, Rebekah could hardly expect to sleep with her forever. But despite her exhaustion, Miriam struggled to drift off, missing the warmth of her sister's body. After losing Karl, it would have meant a lot to her to have felt the closeness of someone she loved.

After breakfast, a young couple came to take Anja and Kathrin to their home.

'We'll be staying in Mile End,' Anja said, hugging the two girls. Miriam realised she had no idea where Mile End was — and she and Rebekah were about to be taken somewhere in a city about which she knew nothing. Neither could she find out anything until she learned some English.

As a parting gift, Anja gave Miriam a book.

'Kathrin and I won't need this now,' she said as she handed it over, 'but it might help you.'

English for Beginners. Miriam opened the book but the words swam as tears filled her eyes. She'd lost Karl, and now Rebekah was behaving in an inexplicably sullen and sulky way. The only explanation was that the flight from Germany had been more distressing for her sister than she'd supposed. Rebekah had always been disturbed by change and their lives had never known such instability and hardship as during the last year.

'What's that?' Rebekah asked.

'Anja gave me a book so we can learn English.'

'Show me, Mirrie!' Rebekah said, slipping her arm through her sister's. 'We can learn together.' She smiled, the petulant frown had gone.

Perhaps once they were settled, Rebekah's moods would calm down.

* * *

It had only been a small thing but it had hurt Rebekah deeply. For months, she'd walked to and from school with Karl and throughout that time, she'd believed him to be fourteen years old — about two years older than her and two years younger than Mirrie, which meant he was the perfect age to be friends with them both.

Indeed, he'd become more than a friend. He was the middle sibling. But now Rebekah had discovered Karl was even older than Mirrie, so the pair of them had more in common with each other than they did with her.

Karl had said nothing to her about the deception and that wouldn't have mattered at all, if he hadn't confided in Mirrie. During the last few months, she'd begun to notice how Karl looked at her sister when he thought he was unobserved and how Mirrie responded. She'd seen how their faces lit up with pleasure when their hands brushed. She'd felt excluded but said nothing.

She adored them both but when she discovered they had a secret they'd kept from her, she'd been crushed. Of course, she'd been desperately sorry when they'd been told Karl had missed the ferry crossing, particularly knowing that if he hadn't tried to find her some food, he'd be with them in England now. Yes, she felt guilty about that, but she'd been so hungry. However, Mirrie was acting as though her loss was greater than Rebekah's.

And as for Miriam being so rude to Anja and Kathrin when they'd been so nice! It was hard to understand. She'd wanted to hurt Mirrie and the only way she could think of to do that had been to choose to sleep away from her.

It had been fun, lying next to Kathrin, chatting until they both fell asleep and when she woke in the night and realised her sister wasn't next to her, she'd simply pulled her teddy bear closer.

In the morning, Mirrie hadn't seemed too upset after a night on her own — which was disappointing. In fact, she was acting as if she were in a daze. Rebekah had ignored her during breakfast. She'd sat with Kathrin and chatted to her.

But when the family came to pick up Anja and her sister, Rebekah had suddenly realised that she and Mirrie were the last two refugees in the hostel. Perhaps it was time to make up? After all, she wouldn't be able to manage on her own and already, Mirrie had learned a few English phrases which would be of use.

And Mirrie looked so sad.

Yes, it was time to be friends again.

* * *

Mrs Cohen from the Stepney Jewish Committee arrived some time later with an elderly couple.

'Ah, girls! This is Mr and Mrs Levy. They're taking you to live with them until such time as it's safe for you to return to Germany,' she said.

Mr and Mrs Levy were grey-haired and bright-eyed but although Mrs Levy was dwarfed by her tall husband, it was soon obvious she had the dominant character.

'Such beautiful girls, darling!' she said to Mr Levy. 'And they've come on such a long journey!'

Mrs Cohen insisted all the forms were filled in and signed before she'd allow the eager Mrs Levy to take the two girls from the hostel.

'What are you waiting for, darling! Sign the papers!' Mrs Levy said, taking the girls' hands while Mr Levy completed the paperwork.

Judging by the fur coat and pearls which Mrs Levy wore and her husband's smart suit, they were a wealthy couple.

Miriam bent to pick up the bag and suitcase but Mr Levy insisted on taking them for her and carried them outside to a large, grey car. A group of scruffy boys were admiring it.

'It's a Rover, ain't it, Mister?' one boy called.

'A Rover Sports Tourer, son,' Mr Levy called out. 'I hope you haven't been interfering with it!'

'We wouldn't mess with a beauty like that, Mister,' the boy said.

Miriam was amazed. She hadn't understood what had been said but she could tell it had all been good-humoured. For so long, she'd been suspicious of strangers. She'd feared to go out of the orphanage into the street. No one knew who was a Nazi, who sympathised with their opinions. But here ... it was like being released from a cage.

The Levys' home was not far from the hostel.

'This is Mile End Road,' Mrs Levy said slowly, so they could understand.

Mile End was where Anja said she and Kathrin would be going. It seemed like a point of reference — something at last that Miriam felt was familiar. The house itself was a three-storey building with five large windows on each floor, a large front door and a walled garden with a wrought iron gate. The cook and maid were waiting to greet them in the hall.

With much trepidation, Rebekah started at a local school and found to her delight that she made several friends, all taking it upon themselves to teach her English. Mrs Levy took Miriam with her when she visited her friends but without the constant chatter of a school, Miriam's knowledge of the language lagged behind her sister's.

Much to Mrs Levy's dismay, she started to help Mrs Bolton, the cook and Lottie, the maid, who were both friendly, gossipy women and soon, Miriam's grasp of English improved.

One evening at dinner, Mr Levy was bemoaning the resignation of the chief clerk, Bill, at Levy and Bernstein, the clothing factory he owned with partner Martie Bernstein.

'He's been given a better offer by a rival company! I can't believe it! He's been my right-hand man for fifteen years. Stabbing me in the back, so he is!'

'You'll find someone else, darling!' Mrs Levy said patting his hand.

'People like that don't grow on trees!'

'Well, what about Tom? He's been working for Bill for years. Surely, he knows the job. Why not promote him?'

Mr Levy chewed in silence for a while. 'You know, Hannah, that's actually a very good idea.'

'Of course, it is, darling! Do I ever have anything other than good ideas?'

'I only need to find someone for Tom to train.'

'Exactly!' said Mrs Levy as if talking to a child. 'And I happen to know the perfect person.'

'You do?'

'Of course! Miriam's been helping with the household accounts and I've noticed she's very quick with numbers. She'd be perfect!'

'No offence, Miriam dear,' said Mr Levy, 'but I need someone who can speak very good English and although your understanding has improved greatly — '

'You need someone who's good at numbers. Anything Miriam doesn't understand, she'll soon learn,' Mrs Levy said firmly.

★　★　★

Miriam accompanied Mr Levy to the factory the following day. Tom Maynard was informed he'd be receiving a promotion when Bill left at the end of the week, and he was to teach Miriam as much as he could with a view to her replacing him.

The increased wages and thought of being chief clerk overcame any misgivings Tom had about training a woman to be his assistant. At the end of the week, when Bill took him to the pub to celebrate their new posts, Tom admitted that for a girl — and a young girl at that — she'd picked things up really fast.

The machinists and other women who worked at Levy and Bernstein were suspicious of the new girl at first, begrudging her the position she'd been given. She arrived each morning in Mr Levy's car and the assumption was made that she'd got the job because she was related to the boss.

However, when they discovered from Tom that not only was she good at her job but that she was a refugee who'd fled from Germany on the Kindertransport, they changed their opinion. When

Mr Levy and Mr Bernstein weren't around, they made excuses to go to the office to chat to her and make sure she knew all the latest gossip, which usually entailed Miriam learning new vocabulary and more about the community in which she now lived. If they didn't have a lot to do, they demonstrated their jobs and taught her how to use their machines. Having watched Sister Margarete, Miriam picked it up very quickly.

'You never know if it'll come in handy,' Peggy Towler, one of the machinists told Miriam. 'Once you're married, you'll be able to make your nippers' clothes.'

'Nippers?' Miriam asked.

'Children, kiddies, you know!' Peggy laughed.

Miriam blushed.

'Look at you going red! A good-looking girl like you'll soon have a queue of young men waiting . . . '

And the talk returned to the girls' favourite topic of conversation — men. They told Miriam about the local dance halls and cinemas, and some even offered to set up a date with their brothers. Miriam wasn't sure if they were simply teasing her because she always blushed.

Gradually, she learned more about Stepney, Whitechapel, Limehouse and Mile End and at the weekend, she walked around the district, learning as much as she could about the people of East London. The area wasn't a wealthy one but the people were open and friendly and many had a fierce pride in their Cockney roots.

She often walked through the streets of Mile End, wishing she'd thought to ask the address or even the name of the people Anja and Kathrin were staying with, but it was too late now. Perhaps their parents had come for them. Anyway, it was unlikely she'd ever see them again.

So many people had disappeared from her life. Karl still filled her thoughts, although she never mentioned him. It would be too painful.

She wondered if he'd made it to England. By now, he'd be seventeen and if he'd been held up for some reason, he wouldn't be allowed on the Kindertransport. There was no reason to suppose he hadn't caught the ferry crossing after hers, of course, and she tried to picture him in London, mentally placing him in photographs she'd seen in Mr Levy's newspaper.

She'd only been to central London once. Mr Levy had taken them to a variety show at the London Palladium, near Oxford Street, on Mrs Levy's birthday and Miriam had longed to wander the streets and orientate herself in the city where Karl might now be living.

As soon as Miriam knew the words for writing paper and envelope in English, she'd asked Mrs Levy for some and had written to Sister Margarete. After thanking her for everything, she described their journey to England and how they'd lost Karl at the port in Holland. She wrote about the kind Levys and her new job at the clothing factory.

So, dear, dear Sister Margarete, if Karl writes to you, please send me his address or send mine to him. I would be so happy to know he is safe. Rebekah and I send our love to you and all the children at St Josef's.

All our best wishes,
Miriam Rosenberg

A month later, a letter arrived from Germany for Miriam. Sister Margarete thanked her for the letter and for setting her mind at rest.

The children still talk about you all and often when we are at the dinner table, we wonder where you are and what you are doing. Now, thanks to your lovely letter, we know. Your new home sounds wonderful and you are lucky to have found such good people to take you in.

Sadly, I have heard nothing from Karl. If I do, I shall reply immediately and send him your address. I shall, of course, send you his as well.

You were all such good friends, it is a shame to think of you all in London but not able to see each other. You see that I am assuming that Karl made it to London. I cannot bear to think otherwise.

The morning you left, a letter arrived for Karl from Mr Lindemann's solicitor in London. I sent it back to the office to inform him Karl was no longer with us, but sadly, I cannot remember his name or address or I could contact him to ask if he knows where Karl is. If I had known it would be important, I would have made a note of his contact details. I am so sorry, my dear.

Please keep in touch with all your news.

Every blessing to you and Rebekah, Sister Margarete

Mr and Mrs Levy treated the girls like their own children. Years ago, they'd had a daughter, Bernice, who died in infancy of polio and they had not been blessed with children since. Three framed photographs of a small girl in a flouncy dress stood on the mantelpiece in the living room and with her long, straight black hair and fringe, she looked a little like Rebekah.

Mrs Levy invited the girls to call her and her husband Aunt Hannah and Uncle Harold — unless Miriam was at work, when she was still to call him Mr Levy.

After dinner in the evenings, the family spent time together. Uncle Harold would smoke his pipe and read his newspaper in front of the fire and inevitably fall asleep, while Aunt Hannah sat opposite him doing her embroidery.

Miriam played the piano while Rebekah wrote long entries in the new journal that Aunt Hannah had bought for her and stuck things in her scrapbook. As well as cutting out pictures of flowers and animals, she'd also started to snip out articles about Germany from the newspapers Uncle Harold had finished reading.

Aunt Hannah had been rather disturbed when she realised Rebekah was taking an interest in Hitler's occupation of Czechoslovakia and his threats towards Poland.

'It's not a suitable interest for a young girl, darling,' she'd said to Uncle Harold — but for once, he'd stood his ground and disagreed.

'We don't know what it's like to have lived in Germany. Rebekah does. You have to allow her to find out what's happening.'

Secretly, he was proud of Rebekah's obvious intelligence and inquisitiveness.

'D'you think Hitler will stop trying to take over other countries, Mirrie?' Rebekah asked that night as they got ready for bed. 'You don't think he'll . . . ' Her voice trembled.

Miriam put her arms around her sister.

'Don't worry, Liebling, Hitler will never try to come to Britain. We're safe now.'

'I couldn't bear it if we had to leave here, Mirrie.'

'I know, Liebling, but it'll never happen.'

However, towards the end of the summer, the situation in Europe had deteriorated and on the morning of Sunday, the third of September, the family gathered around the wireless. At quarter past eleven, the BBC broadcast Prime Minister, Neville Chamberlain announcing that a state of war existed between Britain and Germany.

* * *

Shortly after the radio broadcast informing the nation that it was at war, a siren rang out. Aunt Hannah screamed and Uncle Harold led her by the arm into the cellar. Miriam and Rebekah followed with Mrs Bolton and a white-faced Lottie.

Eventually, several hours later, Mr Levy emerged and telephoned the local police station to find out what was happening. It turned out to be a false alarm.

Across the country, preparations

began for war, with gas masks being issued, air-raid precautions and black-out preparations. Men joined the Territorial Army in their thousands; people built air raid shelters in their gardens and then dug up the flower beds and planted vegetables.

For a few months, the girls at Levy and Bernstein chatted about nothing but the war. However when there were no attacks on mainland Britain, the threat seemed to recede slightly and people were even calling the situation the Phoney War.

'My friend's seeing an ARP warden and he said there've been several deaths so far during this war because of the blackout,' Peggy told the others. 'People getting run over by cars or falling down and breaking their necks in the dark!'

Aunt Hannah was determined the girls would enjoy their first Chanukah in London.

'We're going to try to make the girls forget they'd usually spend this time with their parents, darling,' she told her husband. 'With the war hanging over our heads, I think we ought to take every opportunity to enjoy our lives.'

As 1939 drew to a close, Miriam thought back over the changes that had taken place. She now had a new home, a new family and a new job. Rebekah seemed to have settled down and her wilfulness had not returned.

Those were the good things. Yet she missed her parents. No matter how Aunt Hannah fussed over them, it wasn't the same as having Mutter and Vater. She tried not to think of Karl, and scolded herself whenever the pain of separation from him seemed to eclipse the ache of missing her parents. Mutter and Vater had gone but it was reasonable to suspect that Karl was alive and living in London — possibly only a few miles away.

If only Sister Margarete would reply to her letter. Miriam had sent it months ago begging that if Mr Lindemann's solicitor replied, she would forward his address. But there had been no news.

Rebekah said the newspapers were reporting that conditions had deteriorated in Germany, although how the British press could know that for sure, Miriam had no idea. There was no doubt Sister Margarete would be struggling to feed her children and Miriam had asked Uncle Harold how she could send money to St Josef's to help.

Out of her wages, Miriam paid for her keep although Aunt Hannah had been reluctant to take her money. She kept back a small amount for necessary items and the rest of it was deposited in Uncle Harold's bank account.

He told her that when she was older, he'd sort out her own account or suggested that she might like to wait until she married and then her husband would take care of her savings.

The thought of marrying wasn't appealing. For Peggy Towler and the other girls at the factory, marriage was their life's aim but Miriam had experienced so many changes that, now her life had some stability and security, she couldn't imagine wanting to give that up. More importantly, how could she consider another man when her mind only seemed capable of thinking about Karl?

It comforted her to feel the wooden heart nestling between her breasts. No, she didn't want a husband. When she was old enough, she'd manage her own affairs. In the meantime, she'd continue to dream that one day, she'd find Karl.

★   ★   ★

Having successfully occupied Poland, Hitler turned his attention elsewhere and in April 1940, his troops invaded Denmark, then Norway. In May the British Prime Minister, Neville Chamberlain, was replaced by Winston Churchill, who after telling the British people he had nothing to offer but blood, toil, tears and sweat, offered an outline of his bold plans for British resistance.

On the same day, German forces began their assault on Holland and Belgium.

'Oh, Mirrie, look at this,' Rebekah said, pointing out an article in Uncle Harold's newspaper. 'It says the last Kindertransport children have arrived in England . . . there won't be any more now Holland's under German control.'

Both girls were silent for a while, imagining what life might have been like, had they not escaped.

'What's happening to the children who are left?' Rebekah asked.

'I don't know, Liebling.'

Days later, a letter arrived from Spain. It was bad news. Since Germany and England were at war, there was no regular postal service between the two countries, and the letter had been sent by Greta to her cousin in Spain with a request to post it to England. Sister Margarete had developed double pneumonia and had died in March.

While she'd been ill, Greta had looked after all the children and she thanked Miriam for the money she'd sent to St Josef's which had bought much-needed food and coal. Once Sister Margarete had died, the board had closed the orphanage and the children had been sent to different homes. Greta hoped Miriam and Rebekah were happy and that they would remember her fondly.

Later that month, the news was even worse. Thousands of British and Allied troops had been driven back to the French coast by the rapidly advancing German soldiers and were trapped on the beaches of Dunkirk with no means of escape.

Churchill vowed that Britain would never surrender and he set in motion audacious plans to rescue the stranded troops by sending Navy vessels and a flotilla of privately-owned boats across the Channel to pick them up.

It had been a great success, but as Churchill pointed out, 'Wars are not won by evacuations.' With the Germans now as far west as the French coast, the British braced themselves for invasion.

As a result, two thousand men who were classed as 'enemy aliens' were rounded up and interned, including

German Jews who had fled from Europe. It seemed impossible to believe that anyone could consider the people whom the Nazis had persecuted and oppressed could possibly be a threat. Many of the enemy aliens were initially detained in camps and sent to the Isle of Man while others were shipped to Canada.

In July, the SS Arandora Star, a British passenger ship of the Blue Star Line which was carrying many German and Italian internees, was torpedoed by a U-boat off the west of Ireland and sank. Over eight hundred people drowned.

If Karl had made it to London, it was probable he'd been detained and even sent to Canada. It was possible he'd even been on the SS Arandora Star. Miriam couldn't bear to think of it.

Aunt Hannah had asked if Rebekah would like to be evacuated with many of the other children of London but she'd refused to go.

'I love being with you, Aunt,' Rebekah had said. 'I couldn't bear to leave you and Uncle.'

Aunt Hannah tried to persuade her but eventually gave up. Miriam suspected that secretly she was pleased to keep Rebekah with her.

There was another reason for Rebekah to stay. She'd won a place at a grammar school starting in September. Miriam was proud of her and knew Mutter and Vater would have been so too.

Aunt Hannah and Uncle Harold insisted on holding a dinner for the family and a few friends to celebrate Rebekah's success, and it was obvious from the way their eyes lit up whenever they looked at her that they loved her very much.

'When Rebekah starts at her new school, she'll have a lot of homework. We don't want to distract her, so I think it'd be best if Miriam doesn't play the piano or Harold turn on the wireless until she's finished her work,' Aunt Hannah said.

Although Miriam's time on the piano

was now limited, she was happy, knowing that winning a place at the grammar school had increased Rebekah's confidence and determination.

Her little sister was growing up.

5

Karl finally boarded the ferry the day after Miriam and Rebekah had departed. The storm which had raged on the North Sea during their crossing had subsided, although a stiff breeze still blew but from time to time, the sun peeped out from behind the heavy clouds.

He spent the time on deck. Another boy joined him at the rail and tried to start a conversation but Karl felt too miserable to be friendly and after a few attempts, the boy wandered off.

He still couldn't believe how stupid he'd been. If only he'd curbed his temper, he'd be in England with Miriam now. Instead, he had no idea where she was and no prospect of finding her. He would have to wait until she found his letter and contacted him via his father's solicitor.

The clouds at the tail end of the

storm were now only visible on the horizon and although the air was cold, the sun shone as the ferry sailed into the harbour at Harwich.

This is how I'd imagined our arrival in England, he thought. Bright and sunny — but with Miriam, Rebekah next to him on deck, laughing with relief and joy at finally seeing the shores of the country they'd longed to reach. Instead, he stood at the rail surrounded by groups of refugees, who despite their fatigue and sadness were now smiling and chattering excitedly.

He joined the queue to disembark and once in the arrival hall, was told to wait with another group of children who would be going by train to Liverpool Street Station in London.

The man in charge of the group appeared flustered as members of Karl's group disappeared to the toilets and others joined them. Each time the man carried out a head count, the number didn't tally with his list.

'Will you stand still!' he shouted,

trying to raise his voice above the din.

Karl knew there'd be no point asking if he knew who'd have a record of where the refugees from the previous day might have gone. Finally, the frustrated man was satisfied everyone on his list was now assembled in front of him. He bellowed at them to follow him to the station, where he handed them over to a lady from the local Jewish community organisation with enormous relief.

She helped everyone in the group on to the train with their luggage, and found them seats.

'Where's your bag?' she asked Karl. He explained it had been lost. He told her about Miriam and Rebekah and how he hoped his case was with them although he avoided mentioning the scuffle or his interview with the policeman. She'd been on duty the previous day, escorting children to London but she couldn't remember any particular girls, other than the one who'd been sick on the platform.

Karl looked out of the window as the train sped through the Essex countryside. Opposite him, the boy who'd tried to make friends earlier had found someone else to talk to. Karl felt sorry he hadn't made more effort earlier as the boy was obviously nervous, constantly nibbling his nails. But at least, he'd found someone who could offer him more comfort.

When the train arrived at Liverpool Street Station, the lady from the Jewish organisation slipped a few coins into his hand.

'I'm going to be dropping children off in various places now and I know you're familiar with London and are going on your own, but I just thought you might need a few pence to help with the bus fare.'

Before he could thank her, she'd turned and was lining up the children in pairs.

After the relatively quiet life at St Josef's, Karl was initially daunted by the crowds who poured into and out of

Liverpool Street Station. It had been over a year since he'd walked London's busy streets. He had travelled with his father by cab but now, he didn't have money to pay for one.

Ridley and Perkins Solicitors was just off Oxford Street. If he walked, it was possible that by the time he found it, the office would be closed for the day, so he decided to catch a bus.

A lady at the bus stop was very helpful, describing where he needed to get off, how much the fare was, and as the bus came along, she hailed it, in case it didn't stop. Climbing aboard, he found a seat by the window to spot all the landmarks the lady had told him to look out for. The conductor rang the bell and the bus pulled out into the traffic.

'Fares, please,' he called.

Karl had a sudden change of mind.

'Does this bus pass Hatton Garden?' he asked.

'Why? You plannin' a diamond robbery?'

185

The conductor laughed at his joke.

For a second Karl was taken aback. He'd got used to hostility in Germany and it was surprising to have met so many helpful and friendly people since he'd been in London.

The conductor selected the correct ticket and after punching it, he handed it to Karl and told him he'd let him know when to get off.

Karl had often visited Hatton Garden with Vater on his trips to buy pieces of jewellery as investments and as presents for Mutter. It had been on one of those occasions that his father had bought the priceless blue diamond which Mutter had given Karl and which was now sewn into his waistband.

Vater always bought from the same jewellers — Horowitz and Son — because his friend, Manny Horowitz, owned the shop and made exquisite pieces with finest quality diamonds and gems.

He passed St Andrew's Parochial School with the statues — two girls and two boys, one over each of the four doors into the school — and knew that Horowitz and Son, Jewellers, was not much further, on the opposite side of the road.

The bell jangled as Karl entered the shop and Manny's wife, Alice, dusting displays of glittering diamond rings with a feather duster, looked up and smiled politely. It took her a few moments before she recognised Karl, then dropping the duster, she gasped and rushed to embrace him.

'Karl? Karl Lindemann? Oh, how good it is to see you! And such dreadful news about your poor parents! Such sadness. Manny will be thrilled to see you! Come! Come!' She steered him out of the back of the shop to the dusty stairs which led up to the workshop on the first floor and their rooms on the second, all the time asking question after question without giving him time to answer.

'Manny!' she yelled, opening the door to the workshop. 'Come and see who's here.'

About a dozen men sat in the smoke-filled room, hunched over benches, working with tools spread around them covering every surface. A small man in an apron stood up and threw his arms wide in surprise and greeting.

'Karl, my boy! How good to see you!'

Alice took Karl upstairs to the kitchen and made coffee, while Manny sent one of the men into the shop in case a customer came in.

'So, my boy,' said Manny, 'tell Alice and me all about how you've come to be here.'

Karl described how his parents' belongings had been seized after his mother had died, how he'd spent the next few months in an orphanage where he'd been lucky not to have been pressed into working in the mines near Cologne. He told them about the journey by Kindertransport through Holland and the journey by sea to Harwich — although he didn't mention Miriam or Rebekah. Even saying Miriam's name out loud would have been too painful.

Their faces betrayed the empathy they felt, having once been refugees themselves.

'So, who will you be staying with?' Alice asked.

'I don't know. I'd intended to go to Ridley and Perkins first to see if my father has a will there and then see if any of his friends would lend me money for a room. When I get a job, I'll pay them back and of course, if there's money in Vater's bank account in England, I shall inherit that . . . '

'You've only just arrived from the station? And Manny and I are the first people you've visited?'

'Yes, but I must go soon if I'm to get to central London — '

'Nonsense! It'll take longer than a few hours to find one of your father's friends and then get a room. And why would you be on your own after all the terrible things you've been through? You must stay here with us!' said Alice. 'We insist on it, don't we, Manny?'

'Don't let her bully you, my boy!

You're more than welcome here but if you prefer to be with your father's friends, we quite understand.'

'I'd love to stay with you,' Karl said, suddenly feeling very tired.

'Well, that's settled then. I'll get your things,' said Manny. 'Did you leave them in the shop?'

'I don't have anything,' said Karl. 'I lost my case.'

'Then we will look after everything,' said Alice, putting her arm around his shoulder. 'There's no need for you to worry about anything any more.'

* * *

Karl knew that the son referred to in the shop name Horowitz and Son, Jewellers, had died during the Great War although Manny had never altered the sign. Neither did he ever mention the boy who'd died in Northern France in 1918.

Manny and Alice now lavished their love on their daughter, who was the same age as Karl. He vaguely remembered Sarah from his visits to Hatton Garden with his father but she'd been a shy girl. All he could remember was that she'd been smaller than him and plump with a round face and long hair tied back in a thick plait.

They'd never spoken to each other and he'd been grateful that after she'd been summoned to say hello to Karl and his father, she'd always made an excuse to help her mother in the kitchen.

Now, Sarah was as tall as Karl. No longer plump, she was shapely and her face was, if not beautiful, very striking with strong features and bright, intelligent eyes. But the most startling change was in her new self-assurance. Sarah had become a forthright, ambitious young woman.

Manny told Karl that although it was unusual, he hoped his daughter would take over the family business. She showed every sign of being as capable as a son. If one day she married, then perhaps her husband would join her in running the place. Although only sixteen, she'd already shown an interest in jewellery design and Manny proudly displayed her drawings to Karl. She was also adept at ring-making and diamond setting, skills she'd picked up in Manny's workshop.

Initially, she was allowed in with her father's apprentices and craftsmen to sweep and tidy, though she wasn't permitted to touch any tools. A difficult feat in a workshop with so many jewellery-making tools strewn about. She'd kept the room as tidy as she could, washing coffee mugs and emptying ashtrays, but she'd taken the opportunity to watch the craftsmen work, and listen as they instructed the apprentices.

At first, several craftsmen were indignant when Manny allowed Sarah to try her hand at making simple pieces of jewellery, but it became clear that the boss was encouraging her and that if they wanted to remain in favour, they'd better do the same. So they put aside their prejudice and gave her the benefit of their knowledge.

It was grudging at first — it was a waste of their time since she was just a girl, and a spoiled one at that. But when the men saw the delicate work her nimble fingers produced and the intricate designs she sketched, their resentfulness gradually became fierce pride in their unofficial apprentice's creations.

Not only could she make jewellery, but she could also handle the business accounts. It was a job Alice was keen to hand over since her eyesight was not good and keeping the books often gave her headaches, especially when she had to go back over the figures to find a mistake.

Sarah displayed a talent for numbers and reckoning, and it wasn't long before she'd taken over the account books and her mother simply checked the work once she'd finished.

★　★　★

It had taken a week for Karl to visit his father's friends and find Ridley and

Perkins Solicitors. He'd set out the day after arriving at Manny's and had been surprised to find the office just off Oxford Street closed. There was a sign in the window informing potential clients they had moved premises and gave the new address and telephone number, which Karl wrote down.

Their new office was near Hammersmith, and Karl decided that since he was nearer to Mayfair where he and his parents had once rented a house and where most of his parents' friends lived, he'd go there first.

Several of his father's colleagues offered him a place to stay and others offered him a job in their respective businesses but although Mayfair was a far wealthier area than Hatton Garden, Karl was enjoying the bustle of the jewellery district with its constant chatter, hammering and whirr of machines. And of course, Manny and Alice had welcomed him like a long-lost son.

One of Mr Lindemann's friends had warned Karl not to use Ridley and

Perkins for any new work. Mr Ridley had taken time off to convalesce months before and Mr Perkins had not been as conscientious as he should, taking the company to the brink of bankruptcy. When Mr Ridley returned, he managed to head off disaster but a drawback of his rescue scheme had been the sale of the offices in central London and the purchase of cheaper premises. The solicitors had moved all their records and papers to the newly-built office in Hammersmith but one evening, before everything was organised and filed, a fire had broken out in the basement.

It had been rapidly extinguished by the fire service but when the damage was assessed, it was found that boxes and files had been moved and some of their contents tipped out. A few papers were burned and others soaked but most had been untouched. The tidy-up operation had caused severe disruption and many of the remaining clients planned to take their business else-where — as soon as all their records and papers had been found.

Karl was received by Mr Ridley, who offered condolences on the death of his father, news of which reached him shortly after the explosion.

'I'd like to have attended the funeral and, of course, extended my respects to you but after hearing about your father's demise, we didn't hear anything further. How is your mother?'

'There was no funeral,' Karl said and explained about Mutter and the circumstances of Vater's death. 'Didn't you get my letters from Germany?'

'No.' Mr Ridley shook his head sadly. 'I'm so sorry to hear that . . . I'm afraid things haven't been as efficient here as I would have liked and I had no idea about your predicament . . . Unfortunately, I haven't as yet located all your father's papers but I contacted the trustees of the trust fund your father set up for you and they agreed that you will receive a small weekly allowance until your twenty-first birthday, at which time you will inherit the entire amount.'

Not that there was a lot of money in the bank, Mr Ridley stressed. Mr Lindemann had planned to return to Germany and had kept most of his wealth in a bank in Cologne.

The London bank account had been set up to provide sufficient funds for the family to rent their house in Mayfair and live in good style. All that money would eventually be Karl's. As for other assets? Well, unfortunately, until the office was completely organised, Mr Ridley wasn't sure . . .

Karl didn't mention his mother's ring. After all, it didn't really concern the solicitor. His mother had given it to him to use as necessary and he decided that when he got home that evening, he would confide in Manny and see what he advised.

Carefully Karl cut the ring out of his waistband and explained to Manny how his mother had given it to him shortly before she'd died.

'Ah! I remember that diamond well! It's the finest I've ever handled and it cost your father a pretty penny, my boy! D'you want me to put it in the safe for you?'

Manny inspected it with the hand lens he always carried in his pocket and nodded in satisfaction.

'I want to sell it,' Karl said.

'Are you sure?'

'Yes. I want to be able to pay you and Alice for my keep. I've been offered several jobs in offices but I'm not sure that's what I want. I may have to take one of them if I can't find anything else.'

'I'd happily offer you an apprenticeship with me, but I think you may be better off with one of your father's friends . . . '

'I'd love to work here!' exclaimed Karl. 'I love to make things. I'm not cut out to add up figures or file papers.'

'Then you can start tomorrow,' declared Manny. 'And in the meantime, I shall look for the right buyer for your ring.'

★ ★ ★

Karl slipped easily into the routine of Horowitz and Son, and was grateful to Manny and Alice for treating him like a son.

Sarah, however, did not treat him like a brother. She made it obvious she had romantic notions about Karl and if her parents were aware, they made no comment.

Karl suspected that Manny would be very pleased if at some stage in the future, he and Sarah should marry. But romance and marriage were far from Karl's thoughts. Miriam still filled his dreams and he wondered if he would always long for her. One day, he'd have to accept he'd never see her again — but at the moment, he couldn't bring himself to believe she was gone.

He still searched the faces of girls with wavy, black hair in crowds, wondering if luck would throw them together one day. If she'd telephoned Ridley and Perkins at the address on the paper in his suitcase, she wouldn't have received a reply as they'd already moved out. Unless Miriam travelled to the old premises near Oxford Street, she wouldn't find the new address.

And there was no reason to assume she was in London at all. The lady on the train from Harwich had told him that the children who'd arrived on the Kindertransport had been offered homes by families all over Britain. Miriam and Rebekah could be anywhere.

At some stage, he'd have to put Miriam out of his mind. It wasn't fair on Sarah who in her usual direct manner had slipped her hand in his yesterday when they were out running errands for her father. He'd been horrified, but not wanting to hurt her feelings, he hadn't pulled away. He wished now that he had, because it had obviously sent her the wrong signal. When Manny and Alice had gone into the kitchen that night at dinner, she'd moved closer to him, rubbed her leg against his and put her arm around his shoulders.

'Kiss me,' she whispered, turning his face towards hers with her hand on his cheek but luckily, the sound of the kitchen door opening and Alice returning meant she had to move away.

She'd continued to press her leg against his throughout the meal. After dinner, when Manny said he wanted to discuss the sale of the blue diamond ring with him, Karl leapt up eagerly and followed him to the workshop.

He lay in bed that evening, unable to sleep. Tomorrow he would either have to tell Sarah he wasn't interested, which would definitely cause problems. Or . . . He considered the possibility of encouraging her.

War had been declared the previous month and although so far it hadn't made much difference to their lives, it was unsettling to think that Hitler, the man who'd stirred up such hatred of the Jews and others he considered Untermenschen or subhuman, had invaded Czechoslovakia and Poland. It was impossible to believe he might continue to invade other neighbouring countries but then Herr Hitler was an unpredictable dictator. Karl was thinking of joining up, though he hadn't mentioned it to Manny and he wasn't even sure if it would be possible for a German national to enlist in the British armed forces. But it certainly wasn't a time to be considering commitment to one girl. Anyway, he was still too young to consider marriage.

Yet he knew that if Miriam were to reappear in his life, the war and his age would present no obstacle to being with her.

How could he buy himself time and not hurt Sarah's feelings? During the small hours, the answer came to him. He would simply tell her the truth about Miriam and explain he didn't know how long it would take to get over her but if she wanted to wait, then . . . well . . . perhaps . . .

★ ★ ★

Karl's suggestion that he and Sarah go for a walk together in nearby St John's Park had raised her expectations, so when he suggested they sit on a bench, she was almost quivering with excitement. He couldn't look her in the eyes but eventually, he told her about Miriam and how he couldn't stop thinking about her.

Sarah cried, then when she'd got over the shock, she grew angry. How could he have led her on? How could he still be in love with a girl he hadn't seen for nine months? How could he be so cruel? Karl waited silently until her furious outburst was over and once again, she cried.

Passers-by gaped, then walked on, realising the girl was not being threatened. Indeed, she seemed to be getting the better of the poor boy.

When her tears subsided, he held her and tried to comfort her. It hadn't been his intention to hurt her and he wondered if he'd done the right thing.

Eventually, she wiped her eyes, blew her nose and told him she'd wait for him — not forever because, she said pointedly, that would be sheer foolishness, but she'd give him a while to get over the girl. He'd surely come to his senses soon.

They'd returned to Hatton Garden in silence, lost in their thoughts and during the next week, he often caught her looking at him reproachfully as if he were wilfully withholding his affection. But gradually, as time passed, she seemed to be resigned — waiting until he was over Miriam.

In April 1940, German troops marched into Denmark and Norway. Fears that Britain would be next were increased by the presence of around eighty thousand Austrians and Germans now living in the country. The fact that most were refugees who'd fled Nazi persecution in their homeland did nothing to calm suspicions that the so-called enemy aliens were spies assisting Hitler's bid to conquer Europe.

In May, the British authorities began to round up all German and Austrian men over the age of sixteen and intern them in hastily set up camps. Shortly after, a police constable called at the shop, asking for Karl. Sarah and Alice had been in the shop when he entered and in her usual direct manner, Sarah had demanded to know why he wanted Karl.

'None of your business, if you don't mind me saying, miss. Now I'd appreciate it if you'd fetch Mr Lindemann immediately or I may be forced to take you in for obstructing me in my line of duty.'

'Go and get Karl,' Alice said quickly and for once, Sarah didn't argue.

Karl was allowed to gather a few items and then followed the constable along Hatton Garden. He looked back to Horowitz and Son, Jewellers and saw Manny with his arms around Alice and Sarah, standing silently at the door, their faces white with shock. Above the forlorn group, the windows of the workshop were open and craftsmen and apprentices leaned out, watching his arrest in disbelief and dismay.

Three Germans were already at the police station when Karl arrived. Shortly after, they were escorted to an army truck by two armed soldiers and driven to Lingfield Park Race Course in Surrey which had been hastily converted into an internment camp. Karl found himself among fellow Germans, many of whom had once enjoyed careers as doctors, lawyers, professors and scientists. Others were distinguished artists, musicians, writers and sportsmen.

The commanding officer insisted his men treat the prisoners with respect, recognising that most of the internees had good reason to despise Hitler and his views. Although conditions were basic, the worst part of camp life was the boredom.

Within a few days, after morning roll call, the detainees were loaded on to army trucks.

'Where are we going?' one of the men Karl had made friends with asked a guard.

'Pot luck,' said the guard. 'Some trucks are off to Canada, the rest to the Isle of Man.'

'Which trucks are going to Canada?'

'No idea,' said the guard. 'Move along now.'

Karl and his new friend, Nathaniel, climbed into one of the trucks.

'I've always wanted to go to Canada. Just my luck this'll be going to the Isle of Man. What about you, Karl? Where d'you prefer to go?'

'The Isle of Man,' said Karl, not able to consider leaving the country where he believed Miriam still lived.

'Well, one of us'll get our wish!' Nathaniel said.

★   ★   ★

It had been Karl who got his wish.

The ferry docked in Douglas and the men were escorted by armed guards with fixed bayonets to a large Edwardian building which had once been a guest house overlooking the sea but was

207

now surrounded by a double row of barbed wire.

Life in their new 'prison' turned out to be surprisingly pleasant and as Nathaniel commented, 'You could almost imagine you were on holiday — apart from the cold and your snoring, Karl, me old mate!'

After the boredom of Lingfield Park, the men decided that under the lenient commanding officer, they would organise the running of the house and their entertainment themselves.

In June, Italy entered the war and the German internees were joined by a group of Italian men, many of whom had lived and worked in Britain for years. Two of them owned restaurants and they volunteered to prepare the meals, often creating delicious dishes out of the limited rations they were allowed, by adding herbs, spices and other delicacies their womenfolk posted to them.

Others set up a timetable of lessons where those who had special skills taught classes. Karl learned useful phrases in several languages, as well as how to treat cuts and burns, how to mend boots and cut hair. There were many musicians and somehow instruments were acquired, including a piano which one of the internees tuned, and recitals and concerts were held.

Two actors held auditions for parts in Shakespeare's *Twelfth Night* and Marco Alessi, one of the Italians who'd been learning stage set design in London until his arrest, somehow obtained grease-paint for the actors. With clever use of blankets, curtains and other assorted pieces borrowed from guards or intern-ees, he created a set which when the lights were dimmed, removed all trace of the guest house and conveyed the magic of theatre.

Marco and Karl became close friends. For the first time, Karl spoke of Miriam and was surprised that rather than attempt-ing to persuade him to forget her, Marco encouraged him to persevere.

'It must be my Latin blood! It makes me believe in romance and stardust, but if you haven't forgotten her by now, Karl, you're not likely to! Of course, you might find her one day and wonder why you liked her in the first place. But you'll never have peace of mind until you do.'

'But how can I find her? She could be anywhere.'

'Love demands a grand gesture.'

'Such as?'

'I've no idea. I'm a romantic, not a magician!'

That night, Karl lay awake wondering if Manny had been able to sell the blue diamond ring. From time to time, he received letters from Hatton Garden but of course there would be no mention of a sale, assuming one had even taken place. Nevertheless, he trusted Manny and knew he'd do his utmost to get the best possible price.

It appeared that the time Sarah had allowed him to make up his mind had elapsed and she had moved on. In Alice's tactful letters, there was news that her daughter was walking out with the son of a neighbour and reading between the lines, it appeared that she had now set her sights on him. Karl was pleased for her, although it all made him feel as though life was taking place on the mainland and he was being left behind.

As well as stage set design, Marco had studied typography and calligraphy. With his own pens and brushes, he taught Karl how to form beautifully flowing letters with elaborate loops and curls.

The last time Karl had done any lettering had been on Miriam's wooden heart and as he had so many times, he wondered if she still wore it.

Now, with sweeping brush strokes, he recreated the design of the treble and bass clefs which made up the heart and painted the keyboard at an angle across them. Then he took the pen, dipped it in the ink and wrote *Miriam* below the heart. He was so engrossed, he didn't hear Marco approach.

'Did you design that yourself, Karl?'

Karl nodded.

'It's good. Your control of the pen is excellent now. The letters make a very pleasing shape. Since the name begins and ends with M, you can keep going and if you carefully turn the paper and write it in a circle, your final M will be the one you started with. It'll make a wonderful pattern.'

Marco demonstrated on a scrap of paper.

MiriaMiriaMiriaMiriaMiria . . .

It took a lot of practice for Karl to complete a circle of perfectly formed letters and then it occurred to him that as well as forming the letters into a circle, he could outline the heart in a similar manner. When he'd finished, he stuck it on the wall. Unless anyone looked closely, they wouldn't have known that the outline of the heart was Miriam's name over and over again.

In early July, Marco rushed into the kitchen where Karl was taking his turn helping prepare dinner with the Italian chefs.

'Look at this!' Marco said, spreading

the newspaper on the table and pointing at the headline, *SS Arandora Star
Sunk off Ireland*.

Several days before, the internees had
been asked if anyone wanted to go to
Canada and several had volunteered,
including Nathaniel who Karl had met
at Lingfield Park. He'd tried to persuade Karl and Marco to join him, but
after much thought, they'd decided to
stay.

'We could've been on that ship!' Marco
said, aghast. 'So many drowned!'

It had been a tragedy, but public
opinion towards the aliens softened
considerably when the number of dead
became known and the fact that many
of them had been prominent men
who'd been outspoken in their criticism
of Hitler and his Nazi movement. The
following month, those internees who
were categorised as low risk to Britain
began to be released. Karl and Marco
were set free in mid-September and
travelled together to London where
they exchanged addresses.

Karl found a telephone box and called Manny to let him know he was on his way but there was no reply, so he made his way to Hatton Garden. To his horror Horowitz and Son, Jewellers was boarded up. The roof was missing and the charred beams showed that there had been a fire in the top floor.

'Got bombed a few nights ago,' a passer-by said, noticing Karl looking at the building. 'If I were you, I'd get a place in a shelter now, mate. They get crowded. The Jerries have been coming over every night for a couple of weeks. No reason to suppose they won't come tonight . . . '

'What happened to the family who live there?'

'No idea, mate,' the man said. 'Sorry.'

6

Hitler's strategic night-time bombing of London and other major British cities started on the afternoon of the seventh of September.

Wave after wave of German bombers targeted industrial and civilian areas, starting in Canning Town and the vital East End docks. It continued throughout the night and the all-clear didn't sound until about twelve hours after the attack had begun. It was the start of what the British press called the Blitz.

Although the population had been prepared for aerial attack, no one had been ready for such ferocious and sustained bombardment.

During the first night of the Blitz, Manny Horowitz's shop was damaged and Levy and Bernstein's clothing factory took a direct hit.

It was lucky it had been a Saturday

afternoon because the factory girls had finished work — but Uncle Harold and Martie Bernstein had both been in the office discussing the equipment they would need for their new order of uniforms.

Peggy Towler had brought the news to Aunt Hannah's house once the all-clear sounded. She lived not far from the factory and had emerged from the shelter to find what remained of her workplace ablaze.

Uncle Harold's sister, Ruth, had arrived and taken control of the situation which was fortunate because Aunt Hannah was not coping with the loss of her husband. When Peggy broke the news, she screamed, her eyes wild and unfocused, until she was exhausted and then she'd gone to bed where she refused to talk or to take food or water.

Miriam and Rebekah had been unable to rouse her and eventually, they'd called the doctor. It was Mrs Bolton, the cook who'd suggested they telephone Ruth Levy.

Miraculously, Uncle Harold's body had been recovered and Ruth arranged the funeral and then the packing up of Aunt Hannah's things.

After the burial, she assembled the cook, maid, Rebekah and Miriam in the sitting room.

'My sister-in-law will need constant care, so I'll take her home with me. I've engaged some men to pack up her belongings and bring them to my house. They will board this house up tomorrow afternoon, so you'll all have time to pack your things. I've written excellent references for you, Mrs Bolton and Lottie. I'm sure you'll find new positions . . . ' She looked at the two sisters. 'And I expect the Jewish Community Organisation will help you two find somewhere to stay — '

'But Miss Levy!' Mrs Bolton said. 'With all the bombed houses, there are so many homeless people, the poor girls won't easily find a place to stay! Isn't there something you can do?'

'I'll have enough on my hands caring

for Mrs Levy. As for the German girls — well, they'll have to take care of themselves, I'm afraid. If you're so keen on helping them, you take them in.'

Everyone was so surprised at the way Ruth's lip curled in distaste when she stressed *German*, that for a second, no one spoke.

'Right,' said Ruth with an air of finality. 'Hannah and I will be leaving shortly. You must be ready to go tomorrow morning.'

The night was spent in the Anderson shelter in the garden, while the Luftwaffe bombers roared overhead, dropping their deadly cargo on London.

'Don't you worry, lovey,' said Mrs Bolton to Miriam. 'We'll find somewhere for you to go. First thing in the morning, I'm sure Mrs Levy won't mind if I use her telephone to call my cousin to see if she's got a room. She lives out in Essex and rents out rooms and you never know, she might have a vacancy. I'm off to stay with my sister in Shropshire and she's only got a tiny cottage, otherwise, you could come with me.'

'And I've got to go back to me mam's house,' said Lottie. 'I've got thirteen brothers and sisters, so you can guess how much room we've got. That is, if the Jerries 'aven't bombed it to bits. It sounds to me like they're dropping bombs over Wapping way tonight.'

The Anderson Shelter was damp and cold and the constant bombing ensured no one slept for long. In the morning, as soon as the all-clear sounded, they emerged tired and dejected.

Miriam had briefly slept but woken with a start on remembering that Uncle Harold had put most of her savings in the bank for her, except twenty pounds which he'd kept in the safe in his office. Uncle Harold had shown her where he kept the key so she planned to find her money before the removal men arrived. If Mrs Bolton couldn't find anyone to take them in, Miriam could perhaps rent a cheap room until she found a job.

When she entered Uncle Harold's

study, she saw with horror that the safe was open — and empty. Ruth must have taken everything.

Miriam and Rebekah walked to Fenchurch Street Station with Mrs Bolton the following morning, picking their way through rubble and debris left by the previous night's aerial attack. Dust, smoke and the smell of burning sugar from the docks filled the air. Lottie had waved goodbye and waited for the removals men to arrive at the house before she left for her mother's in Wapping.

Mrs Bolton had telephoned her cousin to ask about a room and fortunately, one room had recently become vacant.

'Now, don't forget, you need to get off at Laindon. Then out of the station, turn left . . . '

'Keep going and it's the second on the right,' said Miriam with a laugh. 'Don't worry, we won't get lost and there's always the map you drew us.'

Mrs Bolton smiled. 'Yes, I know I'm fussing but I just want you two girls to be settled. How could a lovely kind man like Mr Levy have a sister like that? Chalk and cheese, they are! Now, you've got my address, haven't you?'

Miriam smiled and nodded,

'Good,' said Mrs Bolton. 'Well, as soon as you're settled, let me know, won't you?'

The journey to Laindon hadn't taken as long as Miriam had expected and Mrs Bolton's directions took them directly to a large, shabby house with a sign *Rooms For Rent* in the downstairs window.

The net curtains twitched as Miriam and Rebekah walked up the path and by the time they'd reached the door, a large, barrel-shaped woman was standing at the open door.

'Mrs Munroe?' said Miriam politely.

'Who's asking?' the woman said.

'I'm Miriam Rosenberg and this is my sister Rebekah. Your cousin Mrs Bolton telephoned you this morning to ask if you had a room free . . . '

'You've got an accent,' said the

woman coldly. 'It sounds like a German accent to me.'

'Yes, Rebekah and I are Jewish refugees — '

'You've 'ad a wasted trip. I got no vacancies.'

'But you told Mrs Bolton you had!'

'Not for Germans, I ain't! Sling yer 'ook or I'll call the police.'

She slammed the front door and turned the sign in the window over so that it read *No Vacancies*.

'What are we going to do now, Mirrie?'

Rebekah's eyes were wide in alarm.

'I don't know, Liebling.'

'Perhaps, Mirrie, it might be a good idea if you didn't call me Liebling any more and if we try very hard to lose our accents.'

7

With petrol now rationed, Joanna had considered it rather extravagant to drive the car from Priory Hall to Laindon, so she and her daughter, Faye, had caught the bus. She'd allowed extra time so they could go into the tea room in the High Street for lunch before walking to the station to meet her cousin's children who were going to stay with them for a while.

Eight-year old Faye was buzzing with excitement at the thought of having new people to play with. Joanna's cousin lived with her husband and children in Chelsea but when it became clear the Germans intended to destroy London, she'd asked if fifteen-year old Hannah-Rae and eight-year old Jack could stay with Joanna in Essex. They would arrive on the two-fifteen train from London, giving Joanna and Faye plenty of time to enjoy a leisurely lunch.

'D'you think Jack'll want to play with me, Mama?' Faye asked.

'I'm sure he will, my love, although if he doesn't want to, you must respect his wishes. Remember he and his sister won't see their mother for some time, so he may be a bit unhappy at first.'

Faye's chestnut curls bobbed around her elfin face as she nodded.

'I'll stop Mark from annoying him,' she said pompously. Mark was her younger brother.

'Well, I'm sure you're all going to get on splendidly,' said Joanna. She was tempted to cross her fingers.

Her cousin, Amelia, complained that Hannah-Rae, who apparently now would only answer to the name Rae, had been a wilful child who'd grown into a stubborn and single-minded girl.

Like mother, like daughter, Joanna thought wryly.

Jack was apparently more easy-going although Joanna doubted he would agree to many of Faye's games which usually involved hairdressing or hunting fairies.

From time to time, Amelia's eldest son, Joe, would stay with them. He was going to volunteer to join the RAF and hoped to be stationed at nearby Hornchurch. Life at Priory Hall was about to become very interesting.

Joanna chose a table by the window of Baxter's Tea Rooms so she could keep an eye on the street just in case the Kingsley children arrived early from London. She was reading the menu, when Faye whispered in an urgent voice, 'Mama! Look!'

On the pavement outside the window, a girl had her arm around the shoulders of a smaller girl who was crying. Passers-by paused briefly to stare, and then embarrassed at the scene, moved on.

'Mama! Why isn't anyone helping them?' Faye silently pleaded with her mother to do something.

It was right that a child should care deeply about the suffering of others, and she loved Faye's kind-heartedness, but in this instance, Joanna wondered what she could do. She hurried past the tables in the tea room and rushed outside, half-expecting the girls to have moved on, but they were still there.

'I'm sorry to intrude,' Joanna said softly to the elder girl 'but you seem very upset and I wondered if there was anything I could do to help.'

'I . . . that is, we . . . ' began the taller girl.

Joanna could see she was fighting back tears.

'Well, why don't you join my daughter and me? We're just about to order lunch. You don't have to tell us anything but if we can help, we will.'

Later, Joanna found a telephone box and called her husband, Ben.

'Ben, you wouldn't be a darling and come and pick us up in the car, would you?'

'Isn't the bus running?'

'Probably. Plans have changed a bit . . . '

'Have Rae and Jack arrived?'

'Yes, and they've brought Joe with them.'

'Typical Amelia! Why does she always change things at the last minute?'

'And . . . well, Faye and I've found some girls who need a place to stay for a little while.'

'Girls?'

'Yes — they're German Jewish refugees.'

'How many?'

'Only two. Please say it's all right, Ben! They've had a really awful time and they've got nowhere to stay.'

'Well, of course, Jo. If that's what you want.'

'Yes, that's what I want. So, there'll be seven of us to come home.'

'I hope you know what you're doing, darling. You know Rae's a handful on her own. But throwing two other girls into the mix . . . '

'I know.' Joanna sighed.

The drive back to Priory Hall passed silently, with all the young people crammed in the back and Joanna and Ben in the front, exchanging worried glances.

But after a very quiet dinner, Ben suggested playing cards and gradually, the conversation began to flow. Rae was fascinated to learn that Miriam and Rebekah had fled on the Kindertransport from Germany.

'When I'm grown up and this stupid war is over, I'm going to travel all round the world,' she declared. 'I might not go to Germany though — I hope you don't mind me saying.'

'I doubt Bekah and I shall ever go back,' said Miriam. 'There are too many bad memories.' She briefly touched the wooden heart which was hidden inside her blouse.

Faye was fascinated by Rebekah, who was closer to her age than the other girls, and offered to plait her long straight hair.

Jack, as Amelia had described, was a

happy-go-lucky boy who didn't look as though he was going to be any trouble and Joe was only staying for two nights.

'I think we'll survive,' Ben said softly to Joanna that night as they climbed into bed. 'I feel so sorry for Miriam and Rebekah. What terrible lives they've had. I'm proud of you for caring so much, darling.'

★ ★ ★

Rebekah's initial disappointment at not being able to continue at the grammar school was eased by the fact that she was allowed to use Ben's library to supplement her lessons at the local school, where she went with Jack and Faye. When Ben realised how much interest she took in current affairs, he encouraged her, and was amazed at her knowledge of world events. As soon as he'd finished reading the day's newspapers, he gave them to her, often pointing out anything that had interested him.

Rebekah still cut out articles and stuck them in her scrap book and since there were so many people living under one roof, there was always plenty to write in her journal each day.

Miriam and Rae, despite their different temperaments, got on well and both volunteered to work with the Land Army girls on Ben's farm. Rae loved the outdoors life and had soon persuaded Vera, one of the Land Army girls, to teach her how to drive the tractor. She also enjoyed talking to the Italian prisoners of war, who worked on Ben's farm and soon learned a few phrases in Italian.

'Who knows what the world's going to be like when this war's over? But I'm going to learn as many languages as I can,' she said.

Miriam was not so keen on working on the land although she was desperate to pay back Joanna and Ben, and that seemed to be the best way of doing it. But whenever Joanna needed a babysitter for young Mark, or some assistance in the kitchen, she volunteered eagerly and was pleased not to have to do the heavy work that Rae seemed to relish.

One day in late 1941, Joanna's friend, Madeleine, visited Priory Hall. Along with her mother, she owned Maison Maréchal, the most fashionable dress shop in Laindon and she called regularly to chat to Rae in French.

'I'm sorry, Maddie,' said Joanna. 'I think Rae's forgotten.'

'I expect she's having much more fun learning Italian from those handsome prisoners of war!' Madeleine said with a laugh.

'All the same, it's not good enough,' said Joanna with a sigh. 'What a waste of your time!'

'Well, it gave me a chance to drop an advert into the newsagent on my way here. My mother's going away for a few weeks and I'm going to be on my own, so I thought I'd try to get some help while she's gone.'

'What do you need help with?' Miriam asked.

'A little sewing and the accounts. I just can't make all those figures add up.'

Miriam told Madeleine about her experience of book-keeping at Levy and Bernstein's.

'I'm not very good at sewing, though. The factory girls showed me how to use a sewing machine but I wasn't very fast.'

'If you can serve in the shop and look after the books for me, I can probably manage the sewing. And it'll be lovely not to be on my own all day.'

Miriam loved working at Maison Maréchal and was dreading Madeleine's mother coming home, but it seemed she was enjoying her trip and Miriam was thrilled when it was extended by several weeks. Madeleine explained that just before war broke out, Madeleine's mother had met a man in France and fallen in love. He was supposed to join them in Essex but he'd disappeared and hadn't been heard from since.

'Poor Maman,' said Madeleine, 'she

was heartbroken when he didn't come. That's why she's gone away — to try to mend her broken heart.'

'Do you think broken hearts ever mend?' asked Miriam.

'I don't know. Perhaps if she could meet someone else . . .'

Miriam felt sorry for Madeleine's mother. She understood the pain of losing someone. And she was ashamed that she'd selfishly wanted her to stay away so she could continue to work at Maison Maréchal.

Madeleine's words stayed with Miriam. *Perhaps if she could meet someone else . . .*

★ ★ ★

Rae's brother, Joe, had been training to be an RAF pilot for the last few months. He'd recently finished at Elementary Flying Training School and had stayed at Joanna's house whenever he had leave. Joe had matured during the time he'd been away and looked older and more sophisticated than his eighteen years.

The life expectancy of an RAF pilot was measured in weeks and many of Joe's acquaintances adopted a nonchalance and seeming disregard for their lives.

Joe, too, had taken on the devil-may-care attitude and when he'd asked Miriam to go to a dance with him, she'd refused. He hadn't seemed very bothered and she knew he'd simply asked someone else who'd jumped at the chance.

Recently, while Miriam had been playing the piano, he'd let his bravado slip and had told her he enjoyed classical music but didn't dare admit it to his fellow pilots who all liked jazz. He hinted that if she wanted to accompany him to London one evening, they could go to a concert together.

There had been no talk of a specific performance and therefore no dates were mentioned — it was just a possibility — but now Miriam wondered whether she ought to remind Joe in the hope he might take her out.

She couldn't pine for Karl all her life. He was gone, and she had to accept it.

Perhaps someone else would be able to take her mind off him. Madeleine's mother was still sad at her lost love and Miriam couldn't bear to think that when she reached a similar age, she would still be unhappy.

Changes had to be made. She and Rebekah were happy with Joanna and Ben, who'd made it clear the girls were welcome to stay with them for as long as they wanted. It seemed that all the sadness was now behind them. Miriam owed it to herself not to mope any more.

That evening, as she was going upstairs, she met Joe coming down and summoning her courage, she asked him if he still wanted to go to a concert.

Joe had been delighted and promised he'd look out for something they'd both enjoy and get some tickets.

That night, Miriam slipped the red ribbon over her head and cradled the wooden heart in the palm of her hand. After being worn for so long, the paint had faded and the letters on the back were only just visible. *MILD*. She still didn't know what it meant and now, she'd never know. Fighting the feelings of betrayal, she placed the heart in the top drawer of her bedside table.

Without the treasured keepsake it felt as though part of her body had been removed. But she must simply get used to it.

★   ★   ★

Joe and Miriam's first outing together had been enjoyable. He was good company and the concert had been excellent. He'd managed to get tickets to hear Myra Hess, the celebrated pianist, in the National Gallery which had been empty since the evacuation of the artworks several years before. Afterwards, he took her to dinner.

In the restaurant, she noticed heads turn as he led her to a table. Women stared appreciatively, admiring his boyish good looks and men glanced at him enviously. In his RAF uniform, he appeared to be every inch a hero although he seemed oblivious to the attention.

At the table, he had eyes for no one but her, making her feel very special and as the evening progressed and she began to relax, she managed to banish the face that had haunted her thoughts and dreams for the last few years. Joe couldn't have been more different with his piercing blue eyes and his blonde hair with the lock which fell over his forehead despite repeatedly being brushing back. He was handsome and charming. What more could a girl ask?

On the way home, she wondered whether he would kiss her. She both longed for, and dreaded the moment when he took her in his arms when they reached Priory Hall.

When she tiptoed into the bedroom that night, Rebekah was still awake.

'How was your evening, Mirrie?'

'It was wonderful! And Myra Hess was superb!'

Miriam lay awake for several hours. It had been a wonderful evening and the pianist had been superb, just as she'd told Rebekah. She hadn't, of course, told her sister about Joe's goodbye to her. He was expected back at Hornchurch that evening, so he'd driven her to Priory Hall and before she'd got out of the car, he'd put his hands on her shoulders and pulled her gently to him. His kiss had been tender and sweet at first but as she responded, she sensed he was exploring her willingness to go any further and she broke away.

He was disappointed — or perhaps the fleeting expression she'd seen had been annoyance, she wasn't sure. Nevertheless, he'd got out of the car and politely escorted her to the door.

'We'll have to do that again some time,' he said, resuming his casual air.

She'd told him she'd look forward to it. And it was true. The evening had been wonderful.

And yet . . . when she remembered Joe's kiss, she found herself transported back to St Josef's garden with Karl keeping her warm inside his coat, their bodies pressed together. And his lips on hers.

She'd only been kissed twice and common sense told her that they would be completely different experiences. It wasn't fair on Joe to compare. And yet . . .

★ ★ ★

'So, how was the date last night?' Rae asked at breakfast, 'Did my big brother look after you?'

'Yes, it was wonderful,' Miriam said.

Rae looked at her, nibbling her lower lip as if wondering whether to say something. Finally, she made up her mind and said, 'Take care, Miriam. I love my brother dearly but he's a heartbreaker. The trouble is, he's so handsome, he can get away with anything — and he knows it. He's always got his eye out for the next girl.'

'That's a bit harsh, isn't it?'

Rae nodded. 'I probably should've told you before you went but when you said you were going to a classical concert, I didn't realise you were going with him until after you'd gone. Did he behave?'

'He was a perfect gentleman.'

It seemed boastful to say that she hadn't noticed Joe looking at any other girls while they were out. Or perhaps it just seemed naive . . .

Noticing Miriam didn't seem convinced, Rae continued, 'Joe's got the knack of making whoever he's with, feel like she's the most important person in the world. So, there have been lots of them who think he's only interested in them. But the next night, he can be out with someone else giving *her* his undivided attention.

'I think a lot of the RAF lads are like that. They don't know if they're going to see the end of the day, let alone the end of the week, so they feel they need to pack a lot of living into a short space of time. I don't suppose that's what you want to hear, but I wouldn't want you to get hurt.'

Later, when Rae had left to meet the

Land Army girls, Joanna asked how the evening had gone.

She began hesitantly, 'Er, Miriam, I know it's not my place but then again, I don't know whose place it is exactly but . . . that is . . . ' Seeing Miriam's bewilderment, she pressed on. 'Joe is my second cousin and he's a lovely lad. And of course, he's devastatingly handsome. But he's a bit more worldly-wise than you are. I wish I'd thought to say this to you yesterday but . . . well . . . I hope he was a gentleman.'

Miriam smiled. How lovely to have two people looking out for her. She assured Joanna that Joe had been very well-behaved, and that Rae had warned her not to become too attached to him.

'Sometimes Rae's directness is exactly what's required,' said Joanna with a laugh.

* * *

To add weight to Joanna and Rae's words, Miriam didn't hear from Joe for three weeks. When he telephoned, he told her he'd been away training and that he'd got tickets for a night at the Proms — would she like to go with him?

Miriam accepted. After all, she'd had a good time before when he took her out and now both Rae and Joanna had told her what to expect, she was determined not to get too attached to him and make a fool of herself.

Perhaps Rae was wrong. Joe might one day fall for a girl and then be faithful. He would never fill her thoughts like Karl, but she could go out when he was on leave and have a good time.

On the morning of their date, he arrived at Priory Hall to say he had to cancel as he'd been chosen for some special training and he'd be away for a week. He was really sorry but since the tickets were paid for, it would be a shame if they weren't used. Would she like to take someone else?

Miriam knew that Rae preferred Swing music and Madeleine was busy with an order which had to be completed by the following day, so there was no point inviting either of them to the concert.

With a guilty start, she suddenly thought of Rebekah. Since they'd been living at Priory Hall, although the two sisters shared a bedroom, they were not as close as they'd once been. This was the perfect opportunity to re-establish their relationship.

Rebekah was thrilled and Miriam was pleased she'd thought of taking her sister. On the train, she opened the envelope Joe had given her to check the time of the performance on the tickets, but with a start, she saw the venue wasn't the National Gallery as she'd assumed — it was the Royal Albert Hall.

Well, how stupid! Joe had said he had tickets to the Proms. Of course, the performance would be at the Royal Albert Hall!

For a second, she considered telling Rebekah they couldn't go. The Royal Albert Hall was where Karl had promised to take her. But they were already on the train and Rebekah would be so disappointed. Perhaps this was meant to be. It was another step in moving on, and forgetting Karl.

Miriam had left enough time for them to eat first and although she couldn't afford the restaurant where Joe had taken her, she'd been to London several times with Madeleine to buy ribbons and trimmings in a shop near Leicester Square. Afterwards, Madeleine had taken her to Lyons Corner House on the Strand for afternoon tea. Miriam knew Rebekah would love it and that it would remind her of the places Mutter and Vater used to take them to in Cologne, years ago.

'This is so lovely, Mirrie,' Rebekah said, taking her hand as the smartly-dressed Nippy led them to a table and handed them menus.

Since Joanna had taken them in, Miriam's life consisted of her job with Madeleine at Maison Maréchal, helping in Priory Hall and when she couldn't avoid it, working with Rae and the Land Army girls. Rebekah had either been at school, keeping her journal and scrapbook or working in Ben's study.

Miriam realised that recently, her sister had spent more time with Ben, discussing the progress of the war, than with her. Of course, it was good that Rebekah wasn't so reliant on her but she made a mental note to make more time for her sister.

Rebekah needed little prompting to tell her about her school work and how she was learning so much from Ben.

'One day, I want to be a journalist,' she told Miriam, pausing to stare, as if daring Miriam to laugh. 'Well, aren't you going to tell me not to be so stupid?' she added.

Miriam gasped with surprise.

'No! Of course not! Why would I do that?'

'Mrs Thorpe laughed when I told her and said I'd end up getting married like most other women, then all the class laughed too. Except for Jack. When we walked home from school, he said Rae always did what she said she was going to do and that people who thought women couldn't do anything should meet his sister!'

'Teachers should encourage you, not humiliate you in front of the class!' Miriam was outraged. 'Do you want me to have a word with her?'

Rebekah seemed pleased that Miriam had not belittled her dreams and that she was willing to take on the formidable Mrs Thorpe on her behalf.

'No thanks, Mirrie. I've already decided the best way of showing Mrs Thorpe she's wrong, is to *become* a journalist. Imagine how stupid she'll feel then!'

When had Rebekah become so grown-up? Miriam wondered and silently thanked Joe for giving her the means to reconnect with her sister.

The concert in the Royal Albert Hall was thrilling. Karl had described the building to Miriam but her imagination hadn't been able to conjure up anything as spectacular as the sight which met them after their brief walk from South Kensington Station. Rebekah had expected a theatre such as the ones they'd visited in Cologne.

'It's so round, Mirrie! And so enormous!'

During the performance, Miriam closed her eyes and imagined Karl was next to her. How perfect that would have been. But, Miriam decided, if she couldn't be with Karl, it had been marvellous to share the experience with her sister.

8

After Karl returned from the Isle of Man and found that Horowitz and Son, Jewellers had suffered bomb damage, he'd gone to London to see if his father's friend was willing to offer him an advance on his trust money to rent a room.

Max Cavendish, a trustee of his fund and his father's business partner, not only offered him a place to stay but insisted that he join the company.

Karl had accepted both offers gratefully. He'd enjoyed his time working with Manny's craftsmen but he wasn't sure he wanted to start again with someone else — unless of course Manny returned and reopened his shop. But in order to know if that was likely to happen, he had to find Manny.

And then, of course, there was the question of his blue diamond ring . . .

On Saturday afternoon when he'd finished work in the office, he travelled to Hatton Garden where he enquired about Manny in several of the jewellery shops. Many were still open despite suffering broken windows and minor damage during the nightly German aerial bombardment over London. Finally, he found someone who recognised him and was happy to give him Manny's new address in St Albans.

'If you're planning on visiting, you might find a change in poor Manny,' the man cautioned. 'He took the damage to his shop pretty hard. My son, Andrew, is engaged to his daughter and he says Manny's all but given up. Tragic — but it could happen to any of us at any time,' he said, shrugging and looking upwards.

Manny's cottage in St Albans was small but well-kept — not the ostentatious place he'd once laughed about moving to when he was retired. Alice threw up her hands in delight when she found Karl on the doorstep and embraced him warmly. She glanced anxiously over her shoulder before inviting Karl into the cottage, whispering a warning that Manny was not quite himself.

Nevertheless, Karl was shocked. Manny had changed so much, Karl would have walked past him in the street without recognising him. Shortly before the authorities had started arresting all enemy aliens, Manny had celebrated his seventieth birthday. His age had allowed him to avoid detention. But when Karl had left, Manny's thick black hair had been threaded with silver.

Now, it was completely white and his eyes, which had once twinkled, lacked life. He huddled under a blanket, staring into the fire although he looked up when Karl greeted him and it took a second or two before recognition lit up his face.

'Karl, my boy! How good to see you!' His pleasure was obvious but his voice sounded weak as if the effort of speaking tired him.

It was painful to see how such an

energetic, vivacious man had been broken by the destruction of the business he'd considered his life.

Alice insisted Karl stay to dinner, silently pleading with him not to refuse. It had obviously been hard on her to see Manny's decline. During the meal, Sarah arrived. She greeted Karl warmly, making sure he saw her engagement ring.

'I told you I wouldn't wait forever,' she said in tones which suggested she was still aggrieved with him. 'Oh, and by the way,' she added, 'my father's given me the task of selling your blue diamond. As you can see, he's lost interest in the business. I'm running a small shop in St Albans selling the stock we had in London ... Don't worry,' she said when she saw his shock, 'I'll get the best price I can. Although the market's not very buoyant at the moment. But I wouldn't want to *let you down*.' Her expression suggested that was exactly what she wanted to do.

Karl considered asking Sarah for the

diamond ring back but when he'd mentioned it earlier to Manny, he seemed to be under the impression he'd already sold it and paid Karl. There had never been a receipt so if Sarah claimed it was hers, there would be no way of proving who owned it. No — better not to antagonise Sarah further and hope that she would be fair.

It wasn't as though he was penniless. He had a job and soon, he'd inherit the small amount of money in his trust fund. Things could be worse.

Karl was subdued on the train journey back to London. Manny and Alice had offered him so much kindness, treating him like one of the family. What a toll this war was taking. When he finally arrived in London, he was reminded of his return a few weeks before with Marco Alessi. They'd exchanged addresses and promised to keep in touch, although Karl had been so busy settling into his new job, he hadn't contacted his friend. And worse, he remembered he'd given Marco the address of Manny's shop in

Hatton Garden, not realising he wouldn't be returning there.

He found a telephone box and taking the slip of paper out of his wallet, which Marco had given him, he dialled the number.

When Karl heard the familiar gentle Italian accent, he fed several coins into the slot.

'Karl! So good to hear your voice! I telephoned you yesterday but the lines must be down.'

Karl explained about Manny's shop and how he'd just been to St Albans to visit.

'If you hadn't called tonight,' Marco said, 'I wouldn't have been here either. I'm moving out in the morning. I have a new job — and a new room. Have you got a pen?'

Karl wrote down his new address and promised to go the following day to help Marco move in.

★ ★ ★

'Well, what d'you think of my new home?' Marco asked, throwing his arms wide.

Karl had helped Marco carry his things to his new room and been surprised when they'd turned into the elegant street in South Kensington. This was an expensive part of London, but Marco's room was not as impressive as the Regency houses of the street suggested it would be. Access to Marco's new home was down a flight of stairs to the basement. He had his own front door and as the small windows allowed in only a little light, he had plans to paint the entire place in light, bright colours.

Karl told him he was lodging with Max Cavendish, his father's old friend, and Max's wife wasn't happy about it. 'She's the most miserable woman I've ever met,' he said with a laugh.

'Come and share with me!' said Marco. 'I can only just afford the rent. You'd be helping me out. It's near the station so you could get to and from work easily.'

They celebrated with a pint at the

local Prince Albert pub. Marco told Karl about his new job.

'I'm not working on stage set design any more but as soon as a vacancy comes up, my boss says I'll be considered. I'm actually working in the in-house print department, making posters and publicity leaflets. I suppose it makes use of my typography training. It's not quite what I want but a job in the Royal Albert Hall was too good to pass up. And I get cheap tickets, so be prepared to come with me to all sorts of exciting events!'

Karl stared at Marco dumbly.

'Well,' said Marco with a frown, 'I admit, I thought you'd be a bit more enthusiastic.'

Karl explained about his promise to Miriam and how the next time he went to the Albert Hall, he'd hoped he'd be with her.

'Ah, I see. In that case, you're forgiven, but it might be a good way of getting used to the fact she's not part of your life any longer.'

Karl sighed and nodded.

'Yes — I suppose you're right.'

Sharing the room with Karl was working out well, Marco thought. It was just a small place but they were both out all day at work and often in the evening, they went to a performance together.

Marco had set up many double dates for himself and Karl with girls who worked in the Albert Hall. With his Latin charm, girls seemed unable to resist him and he had his pick of the beautiful dancers and singers who appeared on the stage. Karl was polite and engaging but Marco could see he was keeping his distance from them all. His lack of interest only served to make many of the girls keener but once anyone appeared to be getting too attached to him, Karl always finished it.

Marco knew he'd given up trying to find Miriam. But even so, he seemed unable to move on.

One day Alan, his boss, asked him to come up with a design for a poster advertising a piano concert taking place the following month. Sophia Vanelli, a rising star in the music world, would be performing for two nights and Alan was busy with publicity material for a boxing match and a variety show to raise money for the war effort.

'She's a young girl — bubbly, blonde hair, chubby, pink cheeks . . . So, I want something sweet and pretty. Oh, and roses, lots of roses,' Alan said. 'You know the sort of thing . . . '

Marco didn't know the sort of thing. But he was determined to make a good job of it and if it took several designs to get something that pleased Alan, then he'd work all night.

When Karl arrived home, Marco was surrounded by paper and several half-finished designs of roses, pianos, candelabra and sheet music.

'Which one d'you like best?' he asked Karl.

Karl shrugged. 'They're all fine.'

'Fine? Only fine?' He groaned theatrically. 'It has to be perfect! I'll be up all night at this rate.'

Marco had a flashback to the guest house prison on the Isle of Man. Karl had shown him a design he'd drawn for Miriam which had a treble clef on one side and a bass clef on the other.

'You know the design for that heart you once painted for Miriam? Do you still have it?'

Karl nodded.

'Well, will you show me? I've got an idea.'

★　★　★

In the morning, Marco proudly held up the design he'd finished in the early hours. At the top of the poster, he'd written *Sophia Vanelli* in huge, deep pink, loopy script decorated with roses. At the bottom, in the same font and colour, he'd written the performance details and in between, he'd painted an enormous heart formed from a treble clef on one side and bass clef on the other. A simple outline of a young girl with bubbly hair was playing a piano keyboard which lay at an angle across the heart. He'd not painted in the girl's features; nevertheless, with a few brush strokes, he'd managed to capture her completely.

'It's a work of art,' Karl said with admiration.

'It's more than that,' said Marco. 'Look at the outline of the heart.'

Karl stared.

'See,' said Marco, 'it's a love letter!'

He'd written MiriaMiriaMiriaMiriaMiriaM in loopy pink script around the heart. At first sight, it appeared to be lace but closer inspection revealed the name repeated over and over.

'When Miriam sees this, she'll know it's for her,' said Marco. 'She'll contact the Albert Hall and the two of you will be reunited!'

Karl smiled and tried to match his friend's enthusiasm. 'It's wonderful, Marco. Thank you!'

Privately, Karl thought it would be a miracle if Miriam were to spot the heart on a poster but as Marco pointed out, they weren't just put up around the

Albert Hall, they were also on view in train stations and other public places.

'I know you're sceptical, Karl, but I'm Italian and in Italy, we believe in the power of love.'

Love might be powerful, thought Karl, *but it's also heartless and cruel.*

★   ★   ★

'So, did Alan like your poster?' Karl asked Marco that evening when he returned from work.

'He adored it!' Marco said.

'He actually said that?' Karl asked, surprised. He'd met Marco's boss and Alan O'Connor seemed to be a man sparing with his praise.

'Not in so many words,' Marco admitted, 'but he said it would do and I should arrange to get it printed. He wouldn't say that if he hated it!'

'You're such an optimist, Marco!'

Karl was glad his friend's work had been accepted but was worried at the tiny seed of hope starting to sprout inside him. He wasn't sure he could cope with the pain if there was no response.

There was a knock at the door.

'Are you expecting anyone?' Karl asked.

'Only Alan. He's coming round to offer me a promotion and rise in salary.'

Karl was still smiling as he opened the door to find Sarah Horowitz waiting outside in the rain.

'Don't just stand there with your mouth open,' she said. 'Ask me in! I'm getting drenched!'

Hearing a woman's voice, Marco leaped up and began to clear away some of his paint pots and paper from the previous night's art session.

Sarah looked around in disgust at the messy plates in the sink, the pile of dirty washing in the corner and the two unmade beds.

'Bachelors!' she said disdainfully.

'Well, this is a surprise,' said Karl. 'I'm sorry about the mess, but my room-mate, Marco, and I were just about to tidy up.'

Sarah snorted.

'Can I offer you tea?' Karl asked.

Sarah surveyed the cluttered area which served as a kitchen and then at the chairs which were covered in piles of clothes and paint pots.

'No, thank you. My fiancé is outside. We're going to a concert at the Albert Hall. As we were passing, I thought I'd tell you the good news.'

She handed him a bag. Karl's eyes opened wide when he saw bundles of bank notes inside.

'I told you I'd be able to sell your diamond ring,' she said with a satisfied smile. 'There's one thousand pounds in there.'

'One thousand!' said Karl. 'That's all?'

Sarah began to laugh. 'Of course not! What d'you take me for? I'm an expert diamond merchant! Papa told me to give you some cash. He said you had to rely on your allowance and that a large sum might come in handy. This,' she said pulling an envelope from her pocket, 'is a cheque for the balance. And a very healthy sum it is too! By the way, no need to worry about paying me, I've taken my cut already.'

'Your cut?' said Karl with surprise.

'Of course! You didn't expect me to do all that work for nothing, did you? It would've been a different matter if we'd been family — ' she sighed — 'but it was not to be . . . Anyway, you'll be pleased with what I've done with my cut. I've bought a very large house in St Albans, so Andrew and I can marry as soon as we like. It's so large Mama and Papa are going to move in with us. And there'll be room for dogs. Papa always wanted dogs.'

Karl opened the envelope and frowned.

'Yes, that is the correct number of zeroes, Karl. Impressive, eh?'

Karl was speechless.

'Well, I must be off. I expect you've got a lot to think about now. But may I make a suggestion? The first thing I'd do with all that money is engage a cleaner . . . or move out of this dungeon.'

'Dinner's on me!' Karl said, waving the cheque under Marco's nose. 'And I don't mean pie and chips in the Prince Albert!'

★　★　★

'What will you do with all that money?' Marco asked later as they enjoyed steak and chips in a small restaurant they'd often said they'd try when they had some spare cash.

'I don't know. I was beginning to think Sarah would just hold the diamond to pay me back for turning her down, so I didn't want to make plans.'

'I think you had a lucky escape, Karl my boy!' Marco said. 'I wouldn't want to cross swords with her. I pity her poor fiancé!'

Marco laid his knife and fork down and leaned back rubbing his stomach.

'I haven't eaten like that for quite some time.'

Just as the waiter was removing their plates, the air raid siren went off. There were groans as diners rose reluctantly and went out into the street towards the station. ARP wardens shepherded people out of the streets, shouting for calm.

'D'you think we dare make a run for it?' Marco asked, as they queued to go underground. 'We're only a few minutes away from home.'

Karl nodded and together, they ran through the now empty streets back to their basement room. There was an Anderson shelter in the garden but usually, the two men remained in the basement during an air raid.

'You owe me dessert,' Marco said with a laugh.

Karl sighed. 'It would be nice to get through a meal without having to wonder whether the next bomb has your name on it. I'm so sick of this war. I'd never really considered it before because I couldn't afford it but I've always wanted to go to New York. How d'you fancy coming with me?'

'I'm due a few days off soon. I'd love to see New York,' Marco said.

'I'm not suggesting a holiday. I want to go for good. I want to use the money to buy a new start.'

'But what would you do over there?'

Karl shrugged. 'I could ask Max if they need someone to set up a New York office . . . or I could just see what opportunities present themselves. Perhaps we could open up a printing shop.'

Marco shook his head sadly. 'I'd like to go for a holiday but my life is here in London. I'd never get a job as good as the one I've got. There's nothing to rival the Albert Hall in America.'

Karl nodded, 'Yes, I understand.'

'Since you intend to leave me to pay for all this splendour on my own,' said Marco waving his hands around to indicate the room, 'the least you can do is give me your word you won't go until a few weeks after the Sophia Vanelli concerts. Just in case your Miriam sees the poster.'

Now Karl had a plan, he was keen to put it into operation — but it wouldn't hurt to wait a few weeks to please Marco. Anyway, he had to see what Max thought about setting up an office in New York and inform Mr Ridley, his solicitor, that he intended to emigrate.

★   ★   ★

Sophia Vanelli's concert posters appeared on billboards in London and the surrounding areas several weeks before her performance. Had Miriam accompanied Madeleine to her favourite haberdashery shop near Leicester Square, she might have spotted one of them but she had remained in Maison Maréchal to finish Joanna's dress.

Madeleine saw the pink poster with the large heart but took no more notice of it than any other advert in the Underground Station, except she noticed that the concerts were to take place on the same weekend as Joanna and Ben's anniversary celebrations. Her mind was very much on whether she'd be able to get everything she needed and how much there was still to do.

With rationing of material, she'd have to be even more creative than usual, reusing old trimmings and fabric to make wonderful new dresses. And then, of course, there was the question of what she would wear . . .

To Madeleine's relief, all the garments were ready in advance of the big weekend — even her own — and she was able to help out with the food at Priory Hall. The invitation list was enormous and many family members who were travelling from far away were going to stay overnight and go home on Sunday. This was proving to be a problem with the food rationing.

'Never again!' Joanna said the day before the big event. 'My nerves won't stand it!'

But once the party had begun, there were so many willing hands that Joanna began to relax and enjoy herself.

Since Rae spent so much time out on the farm, she knew lots of local people and introduced Miriam to all her friends.

'This is Frank Rigby. He owns a farm in Wickford,' she said, pulling the blushing man towards Miriam. He appeared to be a few years older than her but he had a friendly, pleasant face and when he smiled, his eyes crinkled at the corners, making him seem much younger.

He was obviously not used to mixing with so many people and Miriam felt sorry for him. She, too, was out of her depth but she felt less ill at ease with Frank, especially when she saw Mrs Munroe, the lady who'd refused to allow her and Rebekah to rent a room because they were German, among the guests.

The woman nodded politely when Frank introduced her to Miriam, although she pressed her lips together tightly and Miriam suspected that she didn't approve of a local farmer spending time with a German girl.

At the end of the evening, Frank asked if he could call on Miriam the following day and Rae, overhearing his request, suggested they make up a group and go to Southend-on-Sea 'to blow away the cobwebs' as she put it.

Over the next few days, Frank found time to call either at Priory Hall or Maison Maréchal.

'He's smitten with you, Miriam!' Rae laughed.

Miriam didn't find the situation amusing. She liked Frank well enough but she knew he had feelings for her which she simply couldn't match. It was unkind to give him hope and she decided to let him down gently that evening when he called.

But when he arrived, he was dressed in a suit and told her with such satisfaction that he'd booked a table at a restaurant to surprise her, she felt she couldn't turn him down.

Rebekah lay awake that night, waiting for Miriam to return. She'd said she wouldn't be late but it was now after eleven.

Rebekah didn't like Frank. Not that there was anything wrong with him, but he represented a threat. Exactly what kind of threat, Rebekah couldn't have said. It was just a vague feeling. She and Miriam had been through so much together that the bonds between them were stronger than usual. A man could easily come between them. She'd felt the same about Joe, though it had become clear when she saw him kissing one of the Land Army girls behind the milking shed, that he was not serious about Miriam.

The feelings had started in St Josef's. She'd adored Karl but every so often, he and her sister looked at each other in a way neither looked at her. In fact, they excluded her. Now Frank had started to watch Miriam with puppy-dog eyes. Before long they'd be shutting her out.

Didn't everyone know what a terrible time she and Miriam had shared? No one truly knew how they'd suffered.

Rebekah checked her clock. Eleven-fifteen.

And then she heard the creak of the door as it opened and Miriam tiptoed in.

'I thought you weren't going to be

late!' Rebekah switched on the bedside light.

'Bekah! I'm so sorry, did I wake you?'

'No, I was waiting for you. Why were you late?'

Miriam sighed and sat on the bed.

'I had to choose my words carefully. I didn't want to hurt him but it was so hard telling him in the restaurant.'

Rebekah sat up straight. 'Telling him what?'

'That I can't see him any more.'

'Well, thank goodness for that! He's a drip! What brought you to your senses?'

'Bekah! He's really nice when you get to know him. But he's not for me.'

Rebekah noticed that as she spoke, she placed her hand over where she used to wear the wooden heart beneath her dress.

And that was another thing! Karl had obviously given her that heart, but Miriam had kept it secret from her. She'd never shown her.

That hurt. She knew Karl had given it to Miriam because she'd seen them signal to each other in the orphanage and Miriam placed her hand over it protectively — a gesture she'd continued until Joe asked her out. The wooden heart had been placed in Miriam's bedside drawer beneath a handkerchief, where Rebekah had found it while looking for a pencil. She'd known Karl had given her sister something which hung on a red ribbon but it was the first time Rebekah had seen it.

Lifting it out and turning it over, she'd been impressed by the painting with its treble and bass clefs and keyboard making the design but was puzzled by the word on the other side — MILD.

With a start, she'd realised what it meant. *Miriam Ich Liebe Dich. I love you.*

And that had hurt. Karl had told her he loved her! And Miriam had kept that from her too.

At least now Frank was out of the picture. But she still felt threatened.

★   ★   ★

Rebekah's eyes were swollen when she went down to the kitchen for breakfast. Miriam and Rae had already left for work and Joanna suggested she stay home from school that day.

'Miriam was unhappy this morning and now you look as though you haven't slept. Have you two had a row?'

'Oh no! Well, that is, not exactly . . . '

'Right, I'll make us a cup of tea and if you like, you can tell me all about it . . . '

Rebekah told Joanna about Miriam finishing with Frank and how she thought it a good thing.

'What's wrong with Frank?' Joanna asked. 'He's a pleasant man.'

'Well, I don't like him!'

'But Rebekah, you aren't required to like him. It's between Frank and your sister.'

'It involves me too! I see the way Frank looks at me — he just wants me out of the way.'

'It's not that he doesn't want you

there. He simply wants to be alone with Miriam.'

'He's trying to get between us!'

Joanna sighed. 'I know you're very close to Miriam and you've both been through a lot, but one day, you may decide to go in different directions. You'll still love each other as sisters but you'll both have relationships with other people.'

'No! How will I manage without her?'

'You'll both manage very well. But if one day, Miriam does meet someone she likes, you need to remember that if she decides to be with him, it's not that she's rejecting you. There's room in her heart for lots of people. But at the moment, she hasn't found the right person . . . '

'I think she might have . . . '

Rebekah told Joanna about Karl and how it had been her fault he was not with them on the boat.

'I see,' said Joanna. 'Well, that makes sense. She's seemed adrift since she arrived.'

'But she's got me! She's not adrift at all!'

'Darling, it's not unusual for siblings to be jealous of each other.'

'I'm not jealous! I love Miriam!'

'I think you're jealous of anyone else getting close to her.'

Rebekah was silent for a few minutes.

'What shall I do?' she asked in a small voice.

'Just be the kindest you can be. You're in a much better position than your sister. You have so much to look forward to — you'll pass your exams, go to university if you want to and then I've no doubt you'll make an excellent journalist. Perhaps one day, you'll meet someone and marry. But when Miriam looks into her future, there's very little there — no ambitions, no hope of love if she's still attached to Karl. Just emptiness.'

'I'll look after her.' Rebekah began to cry.

'Yes, I know, darling,' Joanna said and patted her hand, 'but sometimes people need something other than what we can give.'

Rebekah went to her bedroom and closed the door. She pulled out the newspaper cutting from a few weeks ago and tucked it in her pocket with a notebook and pen, then checked how much money she had. She told Joanna she wouldn't be long, then ran down the long gravel drive.

It took her some time to walk to the telephone box at the end of the High Street but she hadn't wanted to waste money on a bus ride. If she had any coins left after she'd made her call, she might be able to catch the bus home.

There was no one in the telephone box. She picked up the receiver and dialled the operator.

'I'd like the Royal Albert Hall, London, please,' she said in her most grown-up voice.

'Certainly, madam, is it the box office?'

'Er, yes, please.' Rebekah had no idea but the box office would be a good start.

'Good morning, the Royal Albert Hall box office, which performance do you require tickets for?'

'Er . . . good morning, I'm phoning about the Sophia Vanelli concerts — '

'I'm sorry, madam, those performances were several weeks ago. We have another piano concert next month. I could give you some details . . . '

'No, it's the Sophia Vanelli concert I need information about — '

'Sorry, madam, I'm afraid I can't help you — '

'Wait!' said Rebekah. 'Don't hang up! I haven't much money and it's a life or death situation!'

'I see. What exactly is it you need to know, madam?' Rebekah could hear the smile in the girl's voice but at least she hadn't hung up.

'I need to know who designed the poster.'

'I'm afraid I have no idea but as it's a life or death situation, the least I can do is try to find out. Please hold the line.'

The girl placed her hand over the receiver but Rebekah could hear the laughter as she recounted the call to the other operators.

Seconds later the girl returned.

'The poster was produced by our own design and printing department. I can put you through if you wish. The manager is Mr Alan O'Connor.'

'Thank you — yes please!'

There was a click and a man spoke.

'Hello, I understand I'm about to be involved in a life or death situation. How can I help?'

There was enough money for Rebekah to explain to Mr O'Connor about how she'd seen the advert for the Sophia Vanelli concert and now desperately needed to contact the artist.

'The poster was designed by my junior, Mr Alessi, but I'm afraid he's out on an errand. Is there a number he can contact you on, Miss . . . ?'

'Miss Rosenberg. I'm in a telephone box. I can give you the number of that.'

'I see, well, read it out, and I'll ask him to telephone when he gets in. He could be a while . . . '

'I'll wait. And thank you, Mr O'Connor.'

'Always happy to oblige in a life or death situation! Goodbye, Miss Rosenberg.'

Luckily no one else wanted to make a call. After an hour of waiting in the cold, the phone rang.

Rebekah lifted the receiver. 'Hello?'

'Miss Rosenberg? It's Marco Alessi. Thank you so much for contacting me . . . '

Rebekah didn't have enough money for the bus fare home, so she walked back to Priory Hall, but it gave her time to think over Joanna's words.

If only she'd acted sooner. After all, she'd found the advert for the Sophia Vanelli piano concert several weeks ago in one of Ben's newspapers and immediately recognised the pattern.

At first, she'd assumed the design Karl had used for the wooden heart was well-known and that the artist had used the same one for the poster, until she'd looked closer with a magnifying glass. Around the perimeter of the heart, she saw *Miriam* written over and over again, as delicate as lace and she'd known that somehow, Karl had found a way of sending her sister a message.

She'd cut the advert out and hidden it in her journal. It would have been a shame to raise Miriam's hopes of finding Karl if it had turned out to be a mistake, she'd reasoned — although now, she was ashamed to admit, she simply hadn't wanted the complication of Karl back in their lives.

But, as Joanna had pointed out, she wasn't required to like anyone Miriam wanted to spend time with. Soon, she was going to make her way in the world and she didn't intend to see Miriam unhappy and directionless. Miriam had been everything to her — a mother, a sister, a friend. The least she could do was try to make her happy.

*   *   *

The letter arrived for Miriam two days later. Rebekah had been looking out for it and she made sure Miriam received it before setting off for Maison Maréchal that morning.

'Who's it from?' she asked casually. 'I don't recognise the writing.'

'I've no idea,' said Miriam. 'I don't recognise it either.' She slit the envelope and pulled out the contents. 'It must be from Joe. I suppose he bought tickets for the Albert Hall and then couldn't make the performance again.'

'Tickets?' said Rebekah, knowing there was only one in the envelope.

'No, I was wrong,' said Miriam, 'there's only one ticket. And there's a note.'

'Who sent it?' Rebekah knew it didn't say.

'How strange. It just says *Please arrive at 1.30pm*. D'you think Joe sent it?' Miriam suddenly froze. 'Or Frank!'

'Oh no!' said Rebekah, afraid Miriam might refuse to go. 'Frank's too stupid to come up with something marvellous like this.'

'Rebekah! That's really unkind! He took me out for a surprise dinner. It's not beyond the realms of possibility he might book a theatre ticket.'

'Yes but . . . ' Rebekah tried desperately to think of something to convince Miriam it wasn't Frank in case she refused to go. 'Anyway,' she said quickly, 'Frank doesn't like classical music.'

'That doesn't mean he wouldn't put up with it for one evening.' Miriam frowned. 'Anyway, how d'you know it's a classical music concert?'

'Oh, silly me! I just remembered, Madeleine told me Frank's asked Martha Timmins to go to a dance on Saturday,' she lied. 'So it looks like he's moved on. I wasn't sure if you'd be upset.'

Rebekah's diversion had worked.

'Upset? No, I'm delighted! Frank's a nice man and I hope he finds happiness.'

'So, you'll go to the concert?'

Miriam looked at the ticket doubtfully.

'No, I don't think so. I think it must've been sent to me by mistake.'

'Oh, but supposing it wasn't? You must go, Mirrie! Just imagine wondering for the rest of your life who sent the ticket!'

'Well, it would be lovely to go to a concert again . . . '

'That's settled then. Why don't you wear that dress Madeleine made for you for Joanna's anniversary party? You look beautiful in that.'

Miriam stared at her sister. 'Really?'

'Oh yes,' said Rebekah, taking her plate to the sink. *Don't overdo it*, she told herself belatedly.

Rebekah told everyone at Priory Hall and Maison Maréchal that a surprise had been organised for Miriam although she wouldn't say what it was, nor who'd made the arrangements. She asked Madeleine to give Rebekah the day off, then warned Rae not to insist she went to help with any farm work. Ben had been warned he must be available at midday to offer Miriam a lift to the station. Joanna had secretly smuggled Miriam's dress out of the bedroom and pressed it. When Miriam was ready, Joanna would suddenly remember she had a bag which matched the dress perfectly and would offer to lend it to Miriam. Faye was thrilled to be asked to brush Miriam's hair and Mark was asked to keep well out of the way with his messy hands.

Rebekah could do no more. It was all up to Miriam now.

★　★　★

'No, I'm sorry, I'm not in the mood. Now I've made my mind up to go to New York, I just want to get on with it,' Karl said when Marco offered him a complimentary ticket to a concert which would take place in three days' time.

'Oh, come on! I paid a lot of money for this!' Marco said, beginning to panic.

'You just told me they were complimentary.'

'What can I say? I lied. They cost me a fortune.'

'I can pay for mine so you're not out of pocket. I'm sure you'll find some female company!'

'I don't know anyone who likes this sort of music.'

Karl looked at the ticket.

'But Marco, you don't like Mozart. I can't understand why you want to go.'

'I don't mind Mozart!' Marco said defensively. 'But I know you like him, so I got the ticket as a goodbye present for you.'

'Oh, I see. Well why didn't you say so? That's really kind. In that case, I'll definitely be there.'

Marco breathed a sigh of relief. Karl had planned to leave the following week, but someone had told him he might be able to get a ticket faster if he actually went to Liverpool and queued up in person.

'What nonsense!' Marco said when Karl told him he was going to pack up and leave immediately, 'Why should you get a ticket any faster by wasting your time queuing up when you can book over the telephone from London? Anyway, I thought you wanted to see Manny before you left.'

'I was going to drop off and see him on my way to Liverpool, but I suppose it would give me longer with him if I spend the day there.'

On the morning of the concert, Marco noticed Karl's bags packed and waiting by the door.

'It looks like you're about to do a runner, Karl! You haven't forgotten about the concert this afternoon, have you?'

'You've been reminding me of nothing else for the last few days! Yes, I'll be there!'

'Twelve-thirty, don't forget. I'll give you a guided tour of the building first. And then I'll buy you our last pie and chips at the Prince Albert.'

Karl laughed and nodded. 'I'm going to miss you and your bossiness like a hole in the head!'

Marco laughed, but he knew Karl well enough to know that was probably the closest he would get to expressing how much he would miss him.

As he left for work that morning, Marco slipped his hands into Karl's bag and withdrawing the wallet which contained all the travel documents and identification papers, he hid it in the inside pocket of his jacket.

Whistling, he climbed the stairs to the road.

★ ★ ★

'I wish you'd tell me what's going on,' Joanna said as Rebekah was putting her shoes on to go to school. 'If you've set up some scheme where you're trying to make amends by getting Frank and Miriam back together, it's going to backfire. Miriam really doesn't want to see him again.'

'Frank? Good gracious, no! This is something Miriam will like . . . '

She broke off. For the first time, she wondered if perhaps it *was* something Miriam would like. She'd never asked her about how she felt about Karl. The more she thought about it, the more she realised she'd made a lot of assumptions.

Suppose Karl hadn't given her the wooden heart? And even if Karl had given it to her, suppose she wore it because it was the only thing Miriam had which linked her to the place they'd once thought of as home? The lack of interest in any other men since they'd arrived in England might be because she simply hadn't met anyone she liked — or perhaps, being older than Rebekah, she'd had greater understanding of all the dangers they'd faced and her emotions had not recovered . . . and would never recover.

Tears came to Rebekah's eyes. She wanted so much to do something nice for Miriam, even though the thought of her sister finding someone special still gave her a momentary stab of fear. She'd lost so much in her short life, it had become second nature to cling on to everything that was precious with all her strength.

And who was more precious than Miriam?

What a terrible catastrophe this war had been! Families torn apart, lives destroyed. But she knew that she and Miriam had been among the lucky ones. They'd been rescued by kind and generous people — from Sister Margarete to the ones who organised the Kindertransport, Uncle Harold and Aunt Hannah and now Joanna and Ben. However, in shouldering the responsibility of looking after her younger sister, Miriam had suffered more.

Now Rebekah wanted to redress the balance. But supposing she'd misread everything and Miriam didn't want to meet Karl? Or worse, suppose she would be keen but he had someone else and wouldn't be interested in Miriam?

She covered her face with her hands and wailed, 'Oh, Joanna, what have I done?'

'You haven't told me, darling! Perhaps it's time you did so we can stop it if we need to.'

Rebekah explained about tracking down Marco Alessi at the Albert Hall and how he was arranging to bring Karl and Miriam together.

'Who is this Marco Alessi?' Joanna asked.

'I don't know! I think he's Karl's friend.'

'But you don't know for sure?'

'No! Oh, Joanna, what shall I do?'

Joanna thought for a moment. 'From

something Miriam said last night, I think she suspects it's Joe who's sent the ticket. If you tell her this is something you set up with a stranger so she can meet Karl, I'm not sure what she'll do. She might go as planned, she might not. But if she doesn't go, she'll always wonder about Karl.' Joanna paused. 'I think the best thing is to let her go. You get off to school and leave the lift to the station to Ben and the bag to me. And then . . . well, we just need to keep our fingers crossed.'

★ ★ ★

'You look like Veronica Lake!' Faye said as she brushed Miriam's wavy hair.

'Veronica Lake's blonde!'

'Well, yes, but you've got the same sort of thick, wavy hair. Anyway, I like your colouring much better. It's so black and shiny. Now, I don't want you going outside and letting the wind blow it about once I've gone to school. It's just perfect now, so keep it nice,' she said, patting it gently.

Miriam smiled and didn't point out that to get to the Albert Hall, she'd have to brave the weather.

'Thank you, darling. You've done marvels. Now, you'd better get off to school. And please keep an eye on Rebekah, she's so jumpy this morning. I don't know what's wrong with her.'

Faye giggled and ran out of the bedroom.

Miriam went down to the kitchen and found Joanna and Mark finishing breakfast.

'What time are you leaving today?' Joanna asked casually.

'As soon as I'm ready. I don't want to miss the bus to town. D'you want me to do anything first?'

'No, I just realised Ben will be back about eleven. I'm sure he'll give you a lift into town and save you waiting for the bus. It might rain later.'

'Oh, I wouldn't want to put Ben out . . .'

'I'm sure it will fit in with his plans just fine.'

'Well, it would be nice to be chauffeured to the station . . . '

'Excellent. Well, that's settled,' said Joanna hastily. 'Oh, and by the way, if you wear that blue dress you wore to my party, I have a bag which would go perfectly with it. And a lovely necklace . . . '

'I haven't really made up my mind.'

'Well, why don't you try the blue one on?'

After breakfast, Miriam put the blue dress on and studied herself in the mirror. The colour suited her and Joanna's necklace set off the neckline perfectly. A wave of sadness washed over her. Mutter had owned many beautiful necklaces; she and Rebekah would have shared them. Now, she had nothing. Not even the pearl earring the police in Cologne had accidentally left her.

She crossed the room and, opening her bedside drawer, she took out Karl's wooden heart. It spun as she held it up by the worn, faded red ribbon.

She'd taken it off in the mistaken

belief that it would be disloyal to go out with a man while still wearing the token of someone she'd once loved.

Once loved? When had she stopped loving him? There had not been any occasion when she had either met someone she preferred or realised her feelings for Karl had gone. So, she must still love him.

But how could you love someone who wasn't there and who you were never likely to see again? It couldn't be love. She was just clinging to memories. She laid the heart in the palm of her hand and looked at its familiar pattern. Hadn't it given her comfort when she'd first arrived in England? It had been her only link with Karl — until it had become a reminder of his absence and then, she'd shut it away and rarely looked at it.

Now she'd accepted Karl was lost to her. He was just a memory — like a candle in a dark room. She slipped the ribbon over her head and tucked the heart inside her dress. If this was all she had left of

Karl, then she would treasure it forever, not hide it away in a drawer.

She decided on the blue dress and when she was finally ready, Ben was waiting in the hall.

'Just in time,' he said. 'I'm about to go into town. Would you like a lift?'

Joanna came in, a struggling Mark in her arms.

'You look beautiful, Miriam. I hope you have a wonderful time.'

*　*　*

Karl arrived in the box office at twelve thirty-five to find Marco pacing up and down.

'Where on earth were you?' Marco asked.

'I'm only five minutes late. I can't find the wallet with my travel documents in. Have you seen it?'

'Um, no. But it can't be far. I'll help you when we get home.'

'I'm sure it was in my bag this morning.'

'It's probably just got pushed under something.'

'But if I can't find it, I won't be able to go.'

'We'll find it. Don't worry,' he said and patted his jacket. The wallet was still in the pocket. 'Now, let's get started, there's quite a lot to see.'

After they'd been in the auditorium and backstage, Marco took Karl to his office. He'd briefly explained to his boss, Alan, that he needed Karl to be kept out of the way while he set up a meeting between Karl and an old friend.

'Ah, this would be the matter of life and death,' said Alan with a laugh. 'So, today's the day for the romantic gesture. Well, you can count on me. I shall bore Karl stupid showing him past posters and if he tries to escape, I'll rugby tackle him.'

Marco wasn't sure Alan was going to take it seriously but when he arrived at the office with Karl, his boss was very polite and started talking about his time in New York several years ago. Karl was so happy listening and asking questions that Marco hoped he'd be able to get his friend out when the time came. He checked his watch. It was eighteen minutes past one. He hurried back to the box office to wait for Miriam.

It occurred to him he had no idea what she looked like. Suppose she'd arrived early and asked one of the staff where she should go, only to be told she was too early for the performance?

'Has a girl come in asking about tonight's performance?' Marco asked the girls at the desk.

'Lots of people,' one said, rolling her eyes. 'This is a box office. That's what people do.'

'No, I mean this girl has a ticket already. But she's been asked to come early.'

The girls shook their heads. One said, 'Is that the girl?' She pointed to a dark-haired girl who was holding a ticket and looking about as if lost.

Marco rushed over to her. 'Miriam Rosenberg?'

She looked at him and smiled. 'Yes . . . ' Then realising she didn't recognise him, she frowned.

'I'm Marco Alessi,' he said, extending his hand, 'and I am here to show you to your seat.'

'But isn't it a bit early?'

'Indeed, it is. But you will be having lunch first.'

'Mr Alessi, do you know who I'll be having lunch with? You see I received this ticket and I don't know who sent it . . . '

'I see. Well, follow me and I'll check in my office,' he said, leading her out of the box office and into the corridor.

For a second, Miriam wondered why Marco Alessi's office was so dark. He'd opened the door for her and gestured for her to go ahead of him.

But it wasn't an office at all.

'Please take a seat at the table, Miss Rosenberg. I shall be back directly.' Marco closed the door behind him, leaving Miriam on her own.

The room was small and lined with

dark, wooden panelling except for the wall ahead of her, which was draped in red, velvet curtains. A gilt-framed mirror hung on one wall and Miriam could see herself in the subdued lighting, her eyes enormous, as she looked about, wondering whether the ticket had, after all, not been intended for her and that it was all a mistake.

The table Marco had referred to was in the middle of the small room and it was laid for two with exquisite crystal glassware, beautiful china and what looked like silver cutlery. Its opulence made the expensive restaurant Joe had taken her look like Baxter's Tea Rooms in Laindon.

The curtains billowed slightly and for a second, Miriam could see through the narrow gap which opened up between them. There wasn't a wall behind the red velvet drapes, as she'd first thought. In fact, there didn't seem to be anything behind them at all. Walking around the table, she gently pulled back one of the curtains and was amazed to see a step down to two chairs, surrounded by a low wall. Suddenly, it all fell into place — she was in one of the grand boxes overlooking the auditorium.

Whoever had arranged this, had gone to a great deal of trouble — and expense. And it obviously hadn't been for her. How disappointed the person who'd paid for this would be when he came and found her, instead of whoever he was expecting. She wondered whether to simply walk out and go home but as she pulled the curtain back into place, there was a tap at the door into the box and it slowly swung open.

The bright light of the corridor flooded in, throwing the two men who stood in the doorway into silhouette. Miriam recognised the small, stocky frame of Mr Alessi, standing slightly behind a taller, slimmer man. Mr Alessi gestured for the stranger to enter and closed the door.

Miriam's eyes, which had adjusted to the dimness of the box, could now see his features. She gasped, her hand flying to stifle her scream.

It was Karl.

Her heart began to race and as her knees almost gave way, she grabbed the back of a chair.

For a second, Karl stood motionless, staring at her as if wondering whether to trust what his eyes were telling him and then, he stepped towards her and placing his hands on her shoulders, he gazed longingly at her face still not quite able to believe she was there.

Her throat was constricted but she managed to whisper, 'Karl!' It sounded like a sigh.

'Miriam?' he said in disbelief. 'How can it be?' He pulled her close, holding her tightly to him and pressing his face against hers, murmuring her name over and over. Feeling moisture on her cheek, she wondered if it was tears from his eyes or hers. Perhaps from both?

He was taller than when they'd held each other so closely in the garden of St Josef's but so was she, and still, their bodies fitted together as if they were two halves of a whole. She could feel his heart pounding, matching hers, and, like her, he was finding it hard to breathe.

Finally, he broke away. Cupping her face in his hands, he looked at her in wonder. 'You're even more beautiful than I remember.' He stroked her cheeks with his thumbs. 'Where have you been, Miriam? How are you? Where's Rebekah?'

But before she could answer any of his questions, he brushed her lips with his and with a sigh of pleasure, she gave herself up to the kiss she'd despaired of ever experiencing again. She closed her eyes, blocking out everything except the pleasure of his lips on her skin as his kisses moved down her neck, to her shoulder and down towards where the wooden heart nestled between her breasts.

A sharp rap on the door jolted them back to the present and Karl stepped away from Miriam, sliding the neck of her dress quickly back into position.

'Good afternoon, sir, madam . . . Luncheon is served,' the waiter announced and then turning around, he took the handle of a trolley. Walking backwards, he wheeled it into the box.

'Madam,' he said, pulling the red, velvet-covered chair out for her to sit down and then after pushing it towards the table, he unfolded a serviette and placed it across her lap.

While the waiter ladled soup into their bowls and offered them bread rolls, Miriam and Karl smiled at each other like naughty children caught stealing biscuits. Beneath the table, Miriam slipped off her shoe and stroked Karl's leg with her foot. His expression showed her that he longed to caress her too and she hoped the waiter wouldn't remain in the box while they ate. But once they'd assured him they had sufficient soup, rolls and wine, he bowed slightly and announced he would return for their bowls and serve the main course once he'd attended to the guests in the neighbouring box.

With regular interruptions by the waiter, they knew there would be no further opportunity to embrace until the meal was over, so they told each other what had happened after Karl left to find more cake for Rebekah at the Hook of Holland.

Karl described how, in his panic at being kept from Miriam, he'd punched the official, his shame at losing control and his despair at finding he'd been left behind. Then he outlined his time with the Horowitz family and his internment on the Isle of Man. Miriam told him about life with Mr and Mrs Levy until the terrible explosion on the first day of the Blitz and how she and Rebekah had been rescued by Joanna.

'But how did all this happen?' she asked, gesturing at the exquisite surroundings of the theatre box. 'How did you arrange it?'

'I didn't. I knew nothing about it. My roommate, Marco, organised everything. Once you contacted him about the poster . . . '

'Poster?' Miriam shook her head. 'I don't know anything about a poster. And I didn't contact him, he contacted me. What sort of poster?'

Karl explained about the design Marco painted in an attempt to trace her and how someone had telephoned to say they knew where she was.

'But I've never shown anyone my wooden heart,' she said with a frown.

The only person who could possibly have seen it was Rebekah. Yet when the sisters first arrived in England, Rebekah had bristled whenever Miriam mentioned Karl's name and several things she had said led Miriam to believe her sister might be more aware of the connection between her and Karl than she'd realised. She thought she'd detected jealousy ... and fear, but wondered if Karl's name brought on feelings of guilt at the thought that she'd triggered the separation. In the end it was safer not to mention Karl at all.

'Well, whoever it was,' Karl said, 'I thank them with all my heart.'

'There is something you can clear up,' Miriam said. Slipping her finger under the red ribbon and lifting the heart out, she placed it in her palm.

'It's a bit faded,' he said, smiling with pleasure that she was still wearing it. 'But I can buy you something much better now . . . '

Miriam shook her head, 'No, no! I love this. But I want to know why you wrote *MILD* on the other side. I've puzzled about that for so long.'

'Ah,' he said with an embarrassed smile, 'that was my way of telling you I loved you without saying the words. *Miriam, Ich liebe dich.* I thought I was so grown up at the time but looking back, I was little more than a boy . . . '

'We were both so young,' said Miriam. 'It all seems like a lifetime ago.'

They held hands across the table, not wanting to lose touch for even a second, anxious for the waiter to clear the table and leave them alone. At last he came and transferred everything to his trolley, drew back the curtains to reveal the auditorium which was beginning to fill up with people and then pushed the trolley out of the box.

306

With a glint in his eye, Karl undid the tasselled tie-backs and drew the curtains, so they were once again unobserved. They moved into each other's arms again and kissed passionately, he holding her tightly, as they had all those years ago. As he nibbled her ear, she threw her head back as waves of pleasure rippled through her.

The members of the orchestra were tuning up and the low hum of people finding their seats in the auditorium gradually increased. When someone coughed nearby, Miriam jumped and Karl broke away from her.

'It's only someone in the next box but perhaps we need to take our seats,' he said reluctantly.

She nodded, not wanting to let him go and hoping they would have an opportunity to hold each other again that evening.

'The night you gave me the wooden heart,' she said, her voice husky with emotion, 'I didn't want you to stop kissing me and I didn't understand why you had. It was quite some time before I realised. But I've marvelled ever since that you could be so considerate. Later . . . when the performance is over . . . ' She struggled to find the words to say she was ready to give herself to him. 'I'm older now . . . and I know what I want . . . I can't imagine ever being without you again . . . '

She wasn't sure she should have said so much and when she saw the look of pain pass across his face, she wished she hadn't. He turned and gestured for her to sit in the viewing area.

What had she said? It had been a moment of rashness. Fancy throwing herself at him like that! But they'd waited so long. Why was it wrong? Unless . . . he wasn't free to love her. After so long apart with no thought of finding each other, it would be perfectly understandable if he was now married. But why had he kissed her so passionately? Perhaps he'd simply been overcome with the emotion of having found her?

He held her hand throughout the

performance but they might as well have been in adjacent boxes for the distance she felt between them.

*   *   *

After the rapturous applause died away and the audience had started to file out, there was a tap on the door. Karl was helping Miriam into her coat and they looked up as Marco poked his head around the door, a huge grin on his face.

'So?' he asked. His grin dropped. Miriam could see he'd detected the atmosphere was strained.

'Yes, wonderful. Thank you, Marco, that was very thoughtful,' said Karl.

'Just thoughtful?' Marco whispered. He sighed as if defeated. 'Oh, by the way, Karl, I went home a short while ago and found this.' He withdrew a wallet from the inside pocket of his jacket and passed it to Karl. 'You'll be wanting it soon, I expect.' He shook his head.

Karl took it and tucked it inside his jacket.

'Well, nice to meet you, Miss Rosenberg,' Marco said sadly and he left.

Miriam walked to the door. It was over.

Karl reached out and closed the door.

'Miriam, there's something I need to tell you.'

She swallowed hard and waited.

'In three days' time, I'm off to New York . . . When you reminded me about that night in the garden in St Josef's, I remembered how I'd always promised to look after you. I couldn't have loved you tonight and then left on Friday.'

'I'm an adult now. It's wartime, people have to take every opportunity to grab happiness — '

'I wouldn't use you like that!' Karl said fiercely.

'So it was just that you're going away?'

He nodded.

'When will you be back?'

He shook his head. 'I won't. I wanted a new start and I suggested establishing a New York office to the board of my

310

father's company. They've bought premises in New York. I'll find staff and set things up. I was told to stay until it's proven to be successful — each trip across the Atlantic is a risk with U-boats sinking so many ships. If I back out, the company will lose a fortune.'

'So I've found you, only to lose you again?'

'Unless — ' his eyes lit up — 'unless you come with me! You said you feel like you're just treading water, why not come with me to New York?'

Miriam shook her head. 'I can't. Rebekah's had such a hard life. I'm the one she relies on.'

'Then bring her too!'

'No, she's settled at Joanna's. She has lots of friends in Laindon and she's set her heart on going to university and then becoming a journalist. I couldn't expect her to give all that up.'

Karl swallowed, 'As soon as I can, I'll come back for you. But will you wait?'

'Yes, I'll wait.'

But, Miriam wondered — in a new

country, with new opportunities and new people — would Karl wait for her?

★ ★ ★

Karl insisted on accompanying Miriam back to Priory Hall, a journey which took place mostly in silence. He still held her hand but there was deep sadness between them. What was there to say?

When they reached the door, Miriam persuaded Karl to go in with her. 'You'll have to spend the night at the station otherwise,' she said, 'there won't be any more trains to London until tomorrow. And anyway, Rebekah will want to see you. She'll be sad if she knows you've been here but didn't wait to see her.'

Miriam left Karl in the large sitting room, on the sofa in front of the dying fire. Unusually, the house was quiet and it appeared everyone had gone to bed early. She crept up the stairs towards her bedroom and quietly opened the door.

Rebekah was sitting up in bed, waiting for her.

'Mirrie! How was it? How's Karl?' she asked eagerly, too late remembering she shouldn't have known Miriam was meeting him.

'It was you who saw the poster!' Miriam said.

'Yes, I saw an advert in Ben's newspaper and I recognised your heart. I'm so sorry, Mirrie, I didn't mean to pry but I wanted a pencil and I didn't know you kept anything special in your drawer. But how was it? Are you seeing Karl again?'

'Come and see for yourself, Bekah. Karl's downstairs waiting to say hello.'

And goodbye, Miriam thought sadly.

Rebekah leaped out of bed and grabbing her dressing gown, ran downstairs to the living room.

'Karl!' She hurled herself at him.

He hugged her. 'I understand Miriam and I have you to thank for bringing us together.'

'Well, it was Mr Alessi really. He made all the arrangements! So, how long are you staying? You are staying with us, aren't you?' Rebekah looked from Miriam to Karl. 'What's wrong?'

Finally, Miriam said, 'Karl wanted to say goodbye to you, Bekah. He has to go away.'

'Away? Where? For how long?'

'I have to go to New York,' said Karl sadly. 'I'll be gone for months, possibly more than a year.'

'So?' said Rebekah, her voice rising in volume and pitch, 'Why can't Miriam go? You can't just leave her behind! Ask her! Go on, ask her!'

'He has asked me, Bekah. But I can't go.'

'You *can't go*?' Rebekah was almost screeching. 'Why ever not?'

'Because I can't leave you behind.' Tears of sadness and frustration trickled down her cheeks.

'Would you go to New York if I came?'

'Of course!'

'Then why didn't you ask me?'

'There's so much for you to give up, Bekah. You know your dream is to go to university and — '

'Miriam!' said Rebekah crossly. 'America has universities and newspapers! It doesn't mean I have to give up my dream. And how d'you think I'd feel, knowing you gave up *your* dream for me?'

'But what about everyone at Priory Hall?'

'We'll miss them but I know they'll understand.'

'So, will you both come with me to New York?' Karl asked, his eyes alight with hope.

Miriam flew to his arms. 'When can we go?'

'Tomorrow?' he asked.

'Tomorrow! Will you have time to get to London to collect your luggage and get back?'

'No. I'm not leaving your side, Miriam, for anything — definitely not for a few cases of clothes. Thanks to Marco, I have my travel documents,' he patted his pocket, 'I'll get clothes and anything else I need when we reach Liverpool . . . after I've exchanged my ticket and bought one each for you two

— on the same crossing this time!'

Miriam's arms were around his neck. Rebekah felt a stab of pain. For so long, Miriam had been hers alone. But Miriam had been willing to give up her chance of happiness for her. How much more proof did Rebekah need of her sister's devotion?

'Right, Mirrie,' said Rebekah loudly. 'I'm going back to bed. I want to be up early to pack, so I'll be fast asleep when you come up. But I definitely won't be down any more tonight . . . Oh, and I suggest you lock the door because the catch isn't good and you wouldn't want it to accidentally bang and wake people. Oh, and there's plenty of coal in the scuttle. Ben filled it earlier. So you won't be cold . . . ' Rebekah pointed theatrically at the lock before letting herself out.

'Is that Rebekah's way of saying she doesn't expect you up to bed immediately?' Karl asked with a smile.

'I think it is,' said Miriam. 'She's become so grown up lately.'

'Now, where were we?' Karl undid the buttons at the back of her dress and slipped it down over her shoulders. 'I think we were about here,' he murmured.

'I don't think we were,' Miriam said with a smile. 'I don't recall you undoing any buttons . . . '

'I was just about to get there, mein Herz.'

As he gently drew his fingertips around her neck and down, following the red ribbon to the wooden heart, she shivered with delight, knowing that from today, they would be together forever.

We do hope that you have enjoyed reading this large print book.

Did you know that all of our titles are available for purchase?

We publish a wide range of high quality large print books including:
Romances, Mysteries, Classics
General Fiction
Non Fiction and Westerns

Special interest titles available in large print are:
The Little Oxford Dictionary
Music Book, Song Book
Hymn Book, Service Book

Also available from us courtesy of Oxford University Press:
Young Readers' Dictionary
(large print edition)
Young Readers' Thesaurus
(large print edition)

For further information or a free brochure, please contact us at:
Ulverscroft Large Print Books Ltd.,
The Green, Bradgate Road, Anstey,
Leicester, LE7 7FU, England.
Tel: (00 44) **0116 236 4325**
Fax: (00 44) **0116 234 0205**

MEDITERRANEAN MYSTERY

Evelyn Orange

Leda unexpectedly finds herself companion to her great aunt on a Mediterranean cruise. Assuming it will be a boring holiday with a crowd of elderly people, her horizons change as she explores the ports of call, and discovers that Aunt Ronnie is lively company. There's also a handsome ship's officer who seems to be attracted to Leda, plus intriguing fellow passenger Nick, who's hiding something. Added into the mix is a mystery on the ship — which becomes a voyage with unforeseen consequences . . .

FIRESTORM

Alan C. Williams

1973: Debra Winters has started a new life for herself as a teacher in a small Australian outback town. Given the responsibility of updating the school's fire protocol, she is thrown together with volunteer firefighter Robbie Sanderson, and there's a spark of attraction between them. Meanwhile, things are heating up: it's bushfire season, and there's an arsonist on the loose. Debra and Robbie find themselves in danger. Will their relationship flicker out — or will they set each other's worlds alight?

A GIFT FOR CELESTINE

Sheila Daglish

The village of St Justin is happy for archaeologist Alex to create a festival exhibition in the chateau beside the Dordogne. The highlight of the display is a fabulous necklace, a gift for a local girl who, centuries ago, was loved by the lord's son. But the jewels bring danger for Alex — and to brooding vineyard owner Raoul. Raw from past betrayals, he denies his attraction to her even as they are drawn closer. But Alex knows there can be no true love, no future, for them without trust . . .

A WOMAN'S PLACE

Wendy Kremer

Sarah Courtney has lived with her aunt and uncle, a prosperous merchant, since her father died a year ago. When the handsome and wealthy Ross Balfour catches her eye, she has no expectation of marrying him — until they accidentally fall into a compromising situation, and he offers for her hand to save her reputation. Ross's plan is for the union to be a sham so that Sarah can receive her inheritance and fulfil her dream of opening an apothecary's shop. Love will never enter into it . . . or will it?